Once Upon Historians

Danika Prasad

Published by Danika Prasad, 2024.

ONCE UPON HISTORIANS

First edition. October 23, 2024.

Copyright © 2024 Danika Prasad.

ISBN: 979-8224795697

Written by Danika Prasad.

Book Praises:

"The book is an adventurous yet mysterious journey, as soon as I read the prologue, I was hooked! To not spoil too much, the book has an eerie feeling to it and is very descriptive!"

~ Friend

"An extraordinary novel, a cross between elements of mystery and history, I would highly recommend this unbelievably amazing piece of literature."

~ Close friend

"This book is monumental! Way more exceptional than I predicted! For someone who has started in her teens and has made it so far, I highly recommend that you give this piece of literature a shot. I guarantee you that you will love it! The moment I entered the world of Historians and opened the pages, I longed to know more!"

~ Friend

"I found the book incredibly well-written, engaging and also informative! Can't wait to read more!"

~ Classmate

This book is a great lesson to follow your dreams and embrace your passions. I love that the descriptions are great, and every character is well thought out!! She has also put a lot of effort into it!

~ Classmate

Acknowledgements:

Writing a book is never a solitary endeavour; it takes the support and encouragement of many individuals along the way. Nevertheless, it has been a lifelong dream of mine and I am deeply grateful to all those who have supported me throughout this journey, including wonderful parents, teachers, friends, and relatives.

First and foremost, I extend my heartfelt appreciation to my supporters, whose unwavering support, guidance, and belief in me made this book possible. Your encouragement fuelled my determination, and I am immensely grateful for your invaluable mentorship.

I would like to express my gratitude to my family for their love, understanding, and patience throughout this journey. Their constant encouragement and belief in my abilities have been a source of strength and inspiration.

To my friends and best friends, thank you for your encouragement, feedback, and support. Your insights and perspectives have enriched this book in countless ways, and I am grateful for your friendship and fellowship.

I extend my sincere thanks to the history teachers who contributed their knowledge and support to this remarkable piece of literature. Their knowledge and insights have been invaluable, and I am grateful for their collaboration.

I am indebted to the editorial and publishing team, who worked tirelessly to bring this book to fruition. Your dedication, professionalism, and attention to detail have been instrumental in shaping this manuscript into its final form.

Finally, to the readers who will embark on this journey with me, thank you for your interest and support. It is my sincere hope that this book will inspire, entertain, and resonate with you in meaningful ways.

With heartfelt gratitude,

Danika Prasad, age 13

Contents:

Prologue (1999):

Amid their picturesque town, enveloped by the serenity of rolling hills and the gentle flow of meandering rivers, the trio's journey unfolded with each step, a symphony of discovery

orchestrating the very essence of their aspirations. Three ambitious 8-year-olds, namely Naureen, Elodie, and Kanchana, fuelled by an unquenchable thirst for knowledge,

ventured further into the labyrinthine depths of history, their hearts pulsating in rhythm with the stories waiting to be unearthed.

Mrs. Khalil, their indomitable guide, led them through dusty archives filled with the whispers of centuries past. Each chapter turned was a gateway to another era, and the trio delved into

the Elodie ls of time with a fervour that transcended the mere study of history; it became an intimate exploration of the human spirit.

Her younger brother, Dr. Hasan, the venerable sage, imparted wisdom that transcended the pages of textbooks. His encyclopaedic knowledge unfolded before them like a vast tapestry,

weaving together the threads of civilizations long gone. With a twinkle in his eye, he regaled them with tales that breathed life into the fragments of history, transforming lessons into

vivid, immersive experiences.

Their expeditions took them beyond the confines of their quaint town. In forgotten corners of ancient ruins and dusty scrolls, they discovered the resonance of lives lived in distant epochs. The past became a living, breathing entity, and the trio found themselves entwined in a dance with centuries-old secrets, unlocking doors to hidden realms where time itself seemed to bend and sway.

As their understanding of history deepened, so too did their bond with each other. Naureen's insatiable curiosity sparked conversations that lingered long into the night. Elodie's meticulous unravelling of mysteries brought clarity to the shadows of the past. Kanchana's eyes, filled with the wonder of ages, reflected the shared awe that enveloped them.

The town, once a backdrop, transformed into a vibrant stage where the unfolding drama of
history played out. The trio, guided by the wisdom of Mrs. Reilly and Dr. Hasan, became the storytellers of their time. Their narratives wove through the tapestry of the town's own
history, breathing life into forgotten tales and shedding light on the extraordinary in the seemingly ordinary.

Yet, their journey had only just begun. A peculiar artifact, discovered in the depths of an ancient crypt, beckoned them towards uncharted territories. It was a key, both literal and
metaphorical, unlocking the doors to a realm untouched by the passage of time. The trio, now inseparable not only by dreams but also by the shared pulse of history coursing through their veins, embarked on a new chapter of their expedition.

The key led them to a hidden library, a sanctuary of forgotten knowledge guarded by ancient tomes. Each volume whispered secrets of civilizations long lost, and the trio revelled in the
intoxicating scent of parchment and ink. Here, amidst the hallowed shelves, they stumbled upon a prophecy—a cryptic verse foretelling an impending shift in the fabric of time.

The prophecy spoke of a cosmic tapestry, threads woven by the hands of destiny itself. It hinted at a convergence of past, present, and future, where the actions of the trio would

resonate across the ages. Intrigued and slightly apprehensive, they realized that their pursuit of knowledge had elevated them beyond the realm of ordinary historians; they were now custodians of a cosmic narrative.

Guided by the prophecy, they began a quest that transcended the boundaries of their town.

Ancient maps and celestial alignments became their guides as they traversed landscapes both physical and metaphysical. Along the way, they encountered enigmatic beings who spoke in riddles and tested the trio's understanding of the intricate dance of time.

Their journey took them to forgotten civilizations hidden in the folds of time, where echoes of their presence rippled through the centuries. They stood witness to pivotal moments, affecting the outcomes of events in subtle yet profound ways. The once quaint trio emerged

as guardians of history, their every step leaving an indelible mark on the tapestry of existence.

As they delved deeper into the mysteries of the prophecy, the fabric of reality itself seemed to unravel. Time, once a linear progression, became a labyrinth of interconnected moments. The trio found themselves confronting their own past and future, unravelling the intricacies of personal destinies intertwined with the grand narrative of the cosmos.

In the climax of their odyssey, they stood at the nexus of time, a crossroads where past, present, and future converged. The key, now imbued with the essence of their journey, resonated with a celestial energy. With a collective breath, they unlocked the final door, revealing a panorama of existence that transcended mortal comprehension.

Their expedition, which began as a quest for historical knowledge, had evolved into a cosmic pilgrimage. The trio, now illuminated by the wisdom of the ages, became custodians not only of the town's history but also of the cosmic tapestry itself. Their story, woven into the very fabric of existence, echoed through eternity as a testament to the boundless possibilities inherent in the pursuit of knowledge and the unravelling of time's mysteries.

Chapter 1: The Ethan Rivers Case:

The daunting mansion of Ethan Rivers casted an eerie glow over the sprawling estate, its
imposing structure a testament to the mysteries that lay within. The floorboards, worn by the passage of time, creaked beneath each step, echoing the tales of forgotten ages that seemed to seep through the very walls. The once young but now aspirational historians stood at the threshold of the mansion's grand library, where the air itself felt charged with the weight of the arcane and the forbidden.

As Naureen's baby blue eyes scanned the immense shelves, they beheld a collection of books that chronicled not just history but the arcane, the mystical, and the forbidden. The man's gaze traversed the room with a mix of anticipation and trepidation, particularly fixated on the volumes dedicated to oral traditions. "Kanchana, Elodie, look at these books. They delve into oral traditions, yet do they truly give a voice to the people it represents?" he pondered aloud.

Elodie Laurent, approaching the enigmatic Ethan Rivers, felt a subtle shift in the air, a tingling sensation that hinted at the potent forces contained within the mansion. As she greeted him, her fingers brushed over the polished wood of the table, revealing a soft, ethereal glow emanating from a crystal ball nestled in a velvet cradle.

"Well, if it isn't those aspirational historians. What brings you here?" queried Mr Rivers.

Visions unfolded before their eyes—long-forgotten civilizations, celestial alignments, and the unforgettable memories of their historical curriculum. A maze of destiny, a tapestry woven by unseen hands, began to reveal itself.

"Hello, Mr. Rivers. I stand here on behalf of all of us, ready to share our opinions and theories," responded Kanchana Desai with valour and confidence.

"Ethan Rivers," the mysterious figure spoke with a haunting whisper, echoing through the

cavernous space. "Not all documents are strictly historical. Oral traditions hold extraordinary events, and you, chosen ones, are destined to navigate the history of oral traditions."

"We stand for you, Elodie," Naureen continued. "Your voice being heard foretells a journey—a journey that will test your intellect, courage, and the very fabric of you." As the figure dissolved into the shadows, Elodie clutched the crystal orb, its pulsating glow mirroring the rhythm of her racing heart. The first page of her theories and explanations had begun, and the pages that awaited her were a tome of uncertainty and revelation.

"Toby, I appreciate the richness of oral traditions in preserving cultural narratives and histories, but it's crucial to recognize their inherent limitations. Unlike written records, oral

traditions rely on human memory, susceptible to distortion over time. Details may be altered, and the core essence of stories can evolve, unintentionally compromising the accuracy of

historical accounts. In a world that values precision, depending solely on oral traditions can be like navigating through a foggy realm where the clarity of historical truths becomes

elusive.

Furthermore, the absence of a tangible, written record reduces accessibility and permanence in preserving historical narratives. Written documents offer a solid foundation for cross-

referencing and verification, ensuring a more reliable preservation of historical truths. While oral traditions contribute greatly, their fluid nature introduces an element of uncertainty.

Embracing a balance between the richness of oral traditions and the reliability of the written word can help us construct a more comprehensive and accurate historical narrative for

posterity."

With the weight of destiny on her shoulders, Elodie's words embarked on a voyage congruent to the expeditions of Vasco de Gama, transcending the boundaries of reason. Little did she know that the echoes of her choices would resonate through time, changing her thoughts and shaping the very course of history.

The mansion's grand library, with its ancient, sentient aura, beckoned Kanchana deeper into the heart of historical knowledge. The towering shelves, approximately 6 feet tall, housed
volumes bound in cracked leather and faded gold, whispering unknown sources to those willing to listen. A chill clung to the air, a testament to the weight of the knowledge held within.

Naureen's footsteps echoed in the vast chamber as he approached an ornate wooden box resting on an intricately carved pedestal. Moonlight filtered through towering windows,
casting intricate patterns on the mosaic floor—a dance of light and shadow, a prelude to the mysteries awaiting revelation.

"Toby, I declare that oral traditions are not reliable. We need scripted documents for
evidence," declared Naureen. The figure, though appearing still, seemed outraged at the perceived belittlement. Kanchana's gloved hands trembled as she gently opened the door,
revealing the crystal orb's soft glow that spilled forth, illuminating the room in hues that defied earthly description.

The orb pulsated with energy resonating with the trio's core. As Kanchana's fingers made contact, visions cascaded through her mind—a torrent of unforgettable dreams revealing civilizations rise and fall, stars converging in celestial ballets, and a prophecy written in the language of
time itself.

"Kanchana Desai, one of the award-winning historians, holder of many theories, you are

chosen. The crystal is your guide through the tapestry of existence. Destiny awaits," echoed a voice in her thoughts. As the visions subsided, Kanchana found herself standing at the nexus of

the extraordinary, surrounded by artifacts and pictures illustrating the captivating mix of Roman, Greek, and Islamic influences.

The silence shattered as a mysterious figure materialized at the library's entrance, cloaked in shadows, their features obscured, exuding an ancient wisdom that transcended time.

Elodie's heart quickened, recognizing the presence of something beyond the realm of mortal understanding.

"Elodie Laurent," Mr. Rivers intoned, their voice weaving through the air like a haunting melody. "You have revealed multiple theories that no one could have thought of. As one of the three chosen award-winning historians, I grant you, Naureen, and Kanchana the treasure of your heart's desire."

The figure continued, revealing the trio's role in an unfolding cosmic drama that extended far beyond the confines of the Daunting mansion. Destiny had woven them into the very fabric of time, and their choices would shape the course of history in ways they had yet to comprehend.

Trio's diary:

Dear Diary,

Elodie :
　Today, Kanchana, Naureen, and I witnessed Ethan Rivers's captivating perspective on oral traditions.
　We engaged in a heated debate, discovering the complexities of giving voice to histories denied.

Naureen:
　Toby's admission about oral traditions not always being sufficient sparked a profound
　conversation among us. It made us rethink the importance of preserving and acknowledging marginalized histories.

Kanchana:
　Seeing Ethan Rivers was truly breathtaking, and our team explored the power dynamics within historical narratives. It's amazing how debates can lead to a deeper understanding of the
　complexities surrounding historical representation.

Chapter 2: Unravelling Mughal Mysteries:

The morning commenced with a sun cast and a warm glow over the iconic Taj Mahal,

historians Naureen, Elodie, and Kanchana embarked on a journey to unravel the secrets of the Mughal era in present times. Affectionately, the historians eagerly stepped into the enchanting world of history that the Taj Mahal held within its marble walls.

Their footsteps echoed through the grand entrance, where intricate patterns and detailed carvings whispered tales of an era long past.

Naureen, with his unrivalled knowledge of architectural history, pointed out, "The nuanced designs truly reflected the craftsmanship of Mughal Artisans."

Elodie , an expert in cultural anthropology, marvelled at the intricate blend of Persian, Islamic, and Indian influences that defined the Taj Mahal.

Kanchana, equipped with her passion for storytelling, envisioned the vibrant court life of the Mughal emperors and their queens as they strolled through the meticulously landscaped gardens. Each step brought them closer to understanding the intricate web of love, politics, and artistic brilliance that defined the Mughal period.

As they reached the main mausoleum, Naureen eagerly shared details about the construction

techniques and symbolism behind the Taj Mahal's majestic dome. Elodie , her eyes gleaming with curiosity, asked probing questions that brought historical nuances to life. Kanchana, capturing every detail with her camera, aimed to preserve the essence of this journey through visual storytelling.

The trio marvelled at the delicate marble inlay work, depicting floral motifs and Quranic inscriptions, as they delved into the historical context provided by Naureen. Elodie couldn't help but be captivated by the tales of Shah Jahan and Mumtaz Mahal's enduring love, which ultimately led to the creation of this timeless masterpiece.

As they moved through the chambers, Kanchana's camera clicked away, immortalizing the rich tapestry of the Mughal era within the digital frames.

"The presence of these three historians transformed the Taj Mahal from a silent monument to a living testament of history," she let out with pride.

Together, Naureen, Elodie , and Kanchana unravelled the layers of time, bringing the Mughal era back to life in the present. The Taj Mahal stood not only as a symbol of love but also as a conduit for these passionate historians to bridge the gap between past and present, ensuring that the

legacy of the Mughal times lived on in the hearts and minds of those who explored its hallowed grounds.

The historians ventured deeper into the heart of the Taj Mahal, discovering a hidden chamber rarely seen by tourists. Naureen, with his keen blue eye for architectural details, noticed a discreet door leading to a secluded space within the mausoleum.

Excitement flickered in Elodie 's hazel eyes as she imagined the stories and mysteries this hidden chamber might hold. Kanchana, eager to capture the unfolding discoveries, adjusted her camera settings to ensure every nuance was immortalized.

Upon entering the secret chamber, the trio found themselves surrounded by exquisite artifacts and relics from the Mughal era. Naureen, visibly intrigued, examined ancient manuscripts and blueprints that shed light on the construction of the Taj Mahal. Elodie uncovered a trove of

personal letters, giving insight into the daily lives and struggles of the Mughal court.

Kanchana, ever the storyteller, envisioned the historical figures coming to life in this intimate

setting. Her camera lens captured the essence of the past, blending seamlessly with Naureen and Elodie 's scholarly observations.

As they delved further, the historians stumbled upon a collection of forgotten portraits. One particularly striking painting depicted a Mughal queen whose story seemed lost to time.

Elodie , determined to resurrect her narrative, meticulously researched, and uncovered the tale of this enigmatic queen, bringing her back into the historical spotlight.

Together, the trio breathed life into the forgotten corners of the Mughal era. Naureen, Elodie , and Kanchana revelled in the joy of discovery, their collective passion turning the Taj Mahal into a

living museum of history. The once-muted echoes of the past resonated through the chamber as they uncovered stories that had long been confined to the shadows.

Their exploration not only enriched their understanding of the Mughal times but also added new chapters to the narrative of the Taj Mahal. As the historians emerged from the hidden chamber, they carried with them not only artifacts and knowledge but also a shared sense of accomplishment, knowing they had contributed to the ongoing saga of this timeless

monument.

With each step, the trio left the hidden chamber behind, but the echoes of their discoveries lingered, intertwining with the ageless tales of the Taj Mahal. The journey through time continued, and Naureen, Elodie , and Kanchana emerged from the depths of history, ready to share their findings with the world.

Trio's diary:

Dear Diary,

Elodie :

The Taj Mahal left us in awe today. The intricate beauty and historical significance of the monument left an indelible mark on our trio.

Naureen:

We marvelled at the artisanry and the love story behind the Taj Mahal. The experience was a testament to the rich cultural heritage that unites people across borders.

Kanchana:

The beauty of the Taj Mahal was beyond words. Sharing that moment with Elodie and Naureen made it even more spectacular.

Chapter 3: Unveiling the Golden Legacy.

In the dimly lit room adorned with ancient maps and crumbling manuscripts, the historians gathered to dive deeper into the enigmatic realms of West African history. The air was
charged with anticipation as they ventured into the Elodie ls of time, weaving together the narratives of Mansa Musa and the intricate trade routes that crisscrossed the continents.

Naureen, the resident expert on West African civilizations, began with an air of excitement, "Our journey transports us to the vibrant lands of West Africa, where Mansa Musa, the
illustrious ruler of Mali, left an indelible mark on history. It was a region pulsating with
cultural dynamism, and much of its wealth stemmed from the abundance of gold that fuelled the trade growth."

Kanchana, leaning forward with intrigue, Interrupted, "Let's not forget the artefacts that were born out of Mansa Musa's era. These relics, adorned with intricate designs and imbued with the essence of West African sophistication, continue to whisper tales of a golden age."

Elodie , her eyes scanning through the thin pages, added, "The trade routes of the time were not merely terrestrial; the waterways served as conduits for commerce, connecting disparate corners of the world. Central Asia, the Silk Road, the Islamic world, and Europe were all linked by a vast network of boat-borne trade, transforming the global landscape."

Naureen interjected, "And in this intricate tapestry of trade, the Mongols played a significant role. Their expansive empire bridged the East and the West, facilitating the exchange of goods, ideas, and cultures along the Silk Road and beyond."

Kanchana, her eyes gleaming with enthusiasm, continued, "West Africa, with its abundant gold

reserves, became a crucial player in this global exchange. Mansa Musa, who ruled Mali in the 14th century, was a central figure in this narrative. His pilgrimage, or Hajj, to Mecca in 1324- 25, became legendary, not just for the religious fervour but also for the staggering display of wealth. With a caravan of 60,000 people and tons of gold, Mansa Musa's journey echoed through Europe, leaving an enduring imprint on the collective imagination."

Elodie mused, "The impact of Mansa Musa's pilgrimage reverberated through the trade routes, shaping the perceptions of West Africa on a global scale. It wasn't just about gold; it was about the interconnectedness of civilizations and the rich cultural exchange that occurred along these maritime and overland routes."

As the historians navigated through the intricate details of West African history, they couldn't help but marvel at the complexities and interconnectedness of the past. Little did they know
that their exploration would not only unearth forgotten tales but also shed light on the enduring legacy of West Africa and the extraordinary ruler, Mansa Musa, who left an indelible mark on the pages of history.

Later in the heart of their scholarly enclave, the trio delved into the rich tapestry of West African history. The room buzzed with excitement as they embarked on a journey through time, unravelling the tales of Mansa Musa and the flourishing trade routes that connected distant lands.

Naureen, with a stack of dusty manuscripts, began, "Our exploration takes us to West Africa, a region teeming with cultural and economic vibrancy. In the 14th century, Mansa Musa, the illustrious ruler of Mali, stood at the epicentre of a kingdom that thrived on trade, notably fuelled by the abundance of gold."

Kanchana interjected, "And let's not forget the artifacts that adorned Mansa Musa's reign, remnants of a golden era. These artifacts, symbols of wealth and sophistication, spoke volumes about the grandeur of West African civilizations."

Elodie , flipping through her notes, added, "Trade, as we know it, was not confined to West Africa alone. The waterways served as conduits for commerce, connecting Central Asia, the Silk Road, the Islamic world, and Europe. It was a time when boats became bridges between distant cultures."

The mention of trade routes led Naureen to elaborate, "The Mongols, known for their vast empire, played a pivotal role in shaping these trade networks. Their influence stretched from the heart of Asia to Europe, creating a dynamic web of economic and cultural exchange."

Kanchana continued, "Much of the gold that fuelled this growth in trade originated from West Africa thanks to Mansa Musa's kingdom. His pilgrimage to Mecca in 1324-25, known as the Hajj, further amplified the fame of Mali's wealth, especially in Europe. It's astounding that even in Europe, tales of Mansa Musa's journey, consisting of 60,000 people and carrying numerous tons of gold, became phenomenal."

Elodie remarked, "Imagine the impact of such a journey on the global perception of West
Africa. The echoes of Mansa Musa's wealth reverberated through the trade routes, leaving an indelible mark on the interconnectedness of civilizations."

As the historians pieced together the puzzle of history, they marvelled at the intricate dance of cultures and commodities across the continents. Little did they know that their exploration would not only illuminate the past but also inspire a newfound appreciation for the golden

legacy of West Africa and the remarkable figure of Mansa Musa.

Trio's diary:

Dear Diary,

Elodie :

So, our attempt at diving into the whole trade, Silk Road, Mansa Musa, and Mali thing turned into this chaotic, delightful mess of interrupted thoughts (how rude) and overlapping ideas.

Naureen:

I mean, Kanchana and I were all hyped about digging into historical trade routes, but the constant back-and-forth, with Kanchana throwing in her facts and theories, turned it into a legit case study. The enthusiasm was real, but let's be honest, Kanchana and my interruptions were like a comedy show—annoying but entertaining, you know?

Kanchana:

True that! Our discussions went off the charts, revealing the crazy connections in global trade. The chaos somehow made the case study kind of fun. But hey, I'll own it – our

interruptions might've been a tad annoying (especially mine), yet they added that touch of lively banter to the whole historical exploration.

Chapter 4: Debating peaks of trade:

The imposing mansion of Janet Abu Lughod stood in the late afternoon sun, casting long shadows over the cobbled path as historians Naureen, Elodie , and Kanchana approached. They had
come together to discuss their latest research on the peak of trade and cultural links between world societies.

Entering the mansion, they found Janet Abu Lughod in her study surrounded by books and artefacts from various eras. The trio exchanged greetings and dived into a passionate debate about which century witnessed the pinnacle of global connections.

"Undoubtedly, it's the 14th century," argued Naureen. "Mansa Musa's pilgrimage to Mecca in 1324 up until 1325 brought unparalleled attention to Mali's wealth, reaching even the ears of European kingdoms. The cultural exchange during this period is unparalleled."

Elodie chimed in, "It wasn't just about Mali. The 14th century saw the rise of the Ming
Dynasty in China, connecting the East and West through the Silk Road. It's a convergence of civilizations that defines the peak of global interaction."

Kanchana added, "Moreover, advancements in maritime technology during the 14th century, like the astrolabe and compass, facilitated long-distance trade, fostering connections between societies that were previously isolated."

Janet Abu Lughod, though appreciative of their arguments, held a different perspective. "While the 14th century indeed witnessed significant global interactions, we shouldn't overlook earlier periods. The 8th to 10th centuries, for instance, were crucial for trade across the Islamic world, connecting Europe, Asia, and Africa through the Abbasid Caliphate."

The debate intensified, each historian presenting evidence from their research. Janet pointed out the importance of the Silk Road during the Tang Dynasty, highlighting the role of the Abbasid Empire as a cultural bridge between the East and West.

As the sun dipped below the horizon, the historians found common ground in acknowledging the complexity of the issue. The interconnectedness of world societies, they realized, was a dynamic and evolving phenomenon that spanned centuries, defying a singular peak.

Leaving Janet Abu Lughod's mansion that evening, the trio, though still with differing opinions, carried a newfound appreciation for the intricate web of trade and cultural links that shaped human history.

The discussions continued late into the evening, the air in Janet Abu Lughod's study thick with the intellectual fervour of historians deeply immersed in their subjects. The trio, now engaged in a lively exchange of ideas, delved into the nuances that defined the peaks of trade and cultural links.

Elodie , with enthusiasm, emphasized the role of cultural diffusion during the 14th century. "Think about it – the exchange of art, literature, and scientific knowledge during this period was unparalleled. The Black Death may have devastated populations, but it also paved the way for a rebirth, a Renaissance that interconnected societies in novel ways."

Naureen, however, brought attention to the intricate trade networks that spanned the globe. "Mansa Musa's pilgrimage was not just a symbol of wealth but also a catalyst for increased trade along trans-Saharan routes. The wealth circulating through these routes connected civilizations in a manner that had never been witnessed before."

Kanchana, ever the pragmatist, interjected, "Let's not overlook the 15th century. The Age of Discovery opened up new maritime routes, forever altering the course of global interactions.

Columbus's voyages to the Americas and Vasco da Gama's journey to India ushered in an era of exploration, forging unprecedented links between continents."

Janet Abu Lughod, observing the passionate exchange, interjected with a thoughtful

perspective. "It's crucial to consider not only the peaks but also the sustained periods of interaction. The Silk Road, for instance, endured for centuries, fostering continuous

connections. We must recognize that the ebb and flow of global interaction is a tapestry woven over time."

As the night progressed, the historians found common ground in acknowledging the cyclical nature of peaks and troughs in global connections. Each century, they realized, contributed uniquely to the ongoing narrative of human interaction.

Leaving the mansion, the trio, despite their initial disagreements, departed with a newfound appreciation for the rich complexities of historical interconnectedness. The question of the

peak of trade and cultural links lingered, prompting further research and exploration into the intricate tapestry of human history.

The next morning, as the sunbathed the world in a new dawn, the historians set out on their individual journeys, armed with fresh perspectives and a shared commitment to unravelling the mysteries of the past.

Days turned into weeks, and the trio continued their research, each delving into their chosen era with renewed vigour. Naureen, driven by the tales of Mansa Musa's opulence, meticulously studied the economic intricacies of Mali's golden age. Elodie immersed herself in the artistic revolutions of the Renaissance, exploring how creativity flowed across borders.

Kanchana, ever intrigued by the Age of Discovery, embarked on a journey through maritime
   records and navigational charts. The trio reconvened at Janet Abu Lughod's mansion, armed with fresh insights and a determination to present their findings.

As they gathered in the study once again, the air thick with the scent of old books and
   parchment, they exchanged the knowledge they had unearthed. Naureen's eyes gleamed with
   excitement as he recounted tales of bustling marketplaces in Mali, where goods from Africa, Europe, and Asia mingled in a kaleidoscope of cultural exchange.

Elodie , with scholarly grace, expounded on the masterpieces of Renaissance art that
   transcended national boundaries. The works of da Vinci, Michelangelo, and Raphael, she

argued, served as cultural ambassadors, carrying the essence of human creativity across the continents.

Kanchana, having traversed the seas through the eyes of explorers, shared tales of uncharted territories and the convergence of diverse civilizations. The exchange of goods, ideas, and
even diseases, she emphasized, shaped a new era of interconnectedness that extended beyond the boundaries of any single century.

Janet Abu Lughod, listening intently to their presentations, smiled knowingly. "History is not a linear progression; it's a mosaic, where each piece contributes to the overall picture. The
peaks we seek are reflections of human endeavours, a culmination of shared experiences that echo through time."

As the discussion evolved, the historians found themselves not in staunch opposition but in harmonious collaboration. They recognized that the 14th century, the Renaissance, and the Age of Discovery were not isolated events but interconnected chapters in the grand narrative of global history.

The evening sun cast a warm glow upon Janet Abu Lughod's study as they concluded their discussion. Leaving the mansion, the historians carried with them not only a deeper
understanding of their subject but also a shared realization that the peaks of trade and cultural links were as diverse and multifaceted as the societies that shaped them.

As they parted ways under the vast canvas of the night sky, the trio looked forward to future collaborations, knowing that the exploration of history's intricate tapestry was an ongoing

journey—one that transcended debates and embraced the collective wisdom of the ages.

Trio's diary:

Dear Diary,

Elodie :
Today unfolded into a thought-provoking journey as our trio engaged in a spirited debate with Janet Abu-Lughod. The topic? Whether the 8th, 10th, and 13th centuries truly represented a peak in trade and cultural links between world societies.

Naureen:
Janet's counterarguments challenged our understanding of historical peaks, prompting us to reevaluate our assumptions. The debate was intellectually invigorating, revealing the intricate nuances of global historical connections. At times, it felt like we were navigating uncharted waters, but the intellectual challenge was refreshing.

Kanchana:
The clash of ideas with Janet added an unexpected dimension to our exploration. We found ourselves grappling with different perspectives, recognizing that historical peaks are complex concepts requiring nuanced consideration. The debate wasn't just a clash of opinions; it was a dynamic exchange that left us with a newfound appreciation for the evolving nature of historical discourse.

Chapter 5: revealing the tapestry of courage.

In the tapestry of historical epochs, our trio of intrepid scholars—Naureen, Elodie , and Kanchana— embarked on an exhilarating expedition to Pennsylvania, traversing the continuum of time to immerse themselves in the extraordinary life of Harriet Tubman. The air was charged with

palpable excitement as they stepped through the portal of history, their senses attuned to the unfolding drama of Tubman's indomitable spirit and clandestine heroism.

The narrative unfurled with a vivid depiction of Tubman's early life, where the stifling atmosphere of enslavement cast a shadow over her formative years. The trio found

themselves captivated by the formidable shackles that bound her, a stark introduction to the crucible from which Tubman emerged with an unyielding determination for liberation.

As they peeled back the layers of Tubman's life, the narrative seamlessly transitioned to the daring chapters of her audacious escape—a cinematic tale of peril and persistence that

whisked the scholars away on a turbulent journey through the labyrinthine landscapes that

defined Tubman's quest for freedom. With each step, they felt the heartbeat of her clandestine journey resonate through the corridors of history, the echoes of her footsteps narrating a story of resilience etched into the very fabric of time.

The spotlight then shifted to Tubman's clandestine masterpiece—the Underground Railroad. In the dimly lit safe houses and secret rendezvous points, the trio experienced the clandestine pulse of a network that symbolized hope and liberation. What began as a historical
exploration transformed into a thrilling adventure, with each clandestine journey akin to a suspenseful chapter in a historical thriller, leaving the scholars on the edge of their
intellectual seats.

Harriet Tubman, the clandestine orchestrator, emerged as a strategic genius in this intricate ballet of liberation. The scholars marvelled at her ability to navigate the clandestine
intricacies, orchestrating clandestine rescues and clandestine forays into the heart of bondage with awe-inspiring finesse. Each clandestine operation unfolded like a symphony of
liberation, challenging the prevailing forces of oppression with clandestine notes that echoed through the ages.

The trio found themselves immersed in the clandestine rendezvous, feeling the hushed
whispers of gratitude and the palpable tension of clandestine journeys towards freedom. The clandestine nature of Tubman's efforts demanded meticulous planning and discreet execution, and she wielded these elements with the grace and precision of a true hero, leaving an
indelible imprint on the historical canvas.

Harriet Tubman's clandestine spirit became a guiding light in the darkness of slavery, a beacon of courage that transcended time. The trio marvelled at her multiple clandestine

forays back into the perilous terrain of bondage, a testament to her unrelenting commitment to leading others towards the radiant promise of emancipation.

As the trio concluded their exploration of Tubman's clandestine exploits, they emerged not only with a profound understanding of her extraordinary life but also a renewed appreciation for the resilience that shapes the course of history. In this monumental chapter, Tubman's

clandestine legacy stood as a testament to the transformative impact of one individual's

courage on the expansive canvas of human history—a clandestine masterpiece woven into the very fabric of time.

The trio, caught in the mesmerizing cadence of Tubman's journey, found themselves

entangled in the intricacies of her clandestine orchestrations. They envisioned the dimly lit safe houses as clandestine sanctuaries, each bearing witness to the courage that pulsed through Tubman's veins and echoed within the clandestine corridors of the Underground Railroad.

The clandestine nature of Tubman's efforts demanded meticulous planning and discreet

execution, qualities she wielded with the grace and precision of a true hero. As the scholars delved deeper into the clandestine symphony of liberation, they marvelled at how Tubman's clandestine notes challenged the prevailing forces of oppression, leaving an indelible imprint on the historical canvas.

Their intellectual sojourn continued as they explored the clandestine rendezvous, sensing the hushed whispers of gratitude and feeling the palpable tension that accompanied clandestine

journeys toward freedom. In those clandestine moments, Tubman's indomitable spirit became tangible, a force that transcended the historical confines and reverberated through the ages.

Harriet Tubman's multiple clandestine forays back into the perilous terrain of bondage emerged as a testament to her unyielding commitment. The trio envisioned Tubman, a

solitary figure navigating the clandestine crossroads of history, leading others towards the radiant promise of emancipation with a fervour that defied the chains of the past.

As the narrative unfolded, the scholars found themselves standing at the crossroads of Tubman's clandestine legacy, a beacon of courage that illuminated the darkness of slavery. With each clandestine revelation, Tubman's clandestine masterpiece painted a vivid portrait of an extraordinary woman who left an indelible mark on the expansive canvas of human

history.

In this monumental chapter, the trio concluded their exploration, not merely armed with a profound understanding of Tubman's life but also infused with a renewed appreciation for the clandestine resilience that shapes the course of history. The clandestine threads of Tubman's

tale had woven themselves into the very fabric of time, leaving an enduring legacy that resonated through the corridors of the past and the uncharted territories of the future.

Trio's diary:

Dear Diary,

Elodie :
Today's adventure in Pennsylvania was like unlocking a hidden treasure of history. Our exploration, especially delving into Harriet Tubman's impactful work, ignited a profound curiosity about the abolition of slavery.

Naureen:
Pennsylvania became a canvas of reflection on Tubman's bravery and the broader history of slavery abolition. The stories we uncovered painted a vivid picture of the struggles and
triumphs that shaped our understanding of justice and human rights.

Kanchana:
Harriet Tubman's legacy resonated deeply with us. Our visit to Pennsylvania wasn't just a stroll through historical sites; it fuelled a collective passion for understanding the
complexities of the abolitionist movement. The journey left us inspired and craving more knowledge about the transformative moments in history that continue to shape our present.

Chapter 6: the legacy of Naureen, Elodie , and Kanchana

In the hallowed halls of historical exploration, flames of inspiration from the esteemed

Manisha Sinha were carried by the beloved trio. Once historians now historical genies, the trio marched forward to the mob of enthusiasm awaiting them.

Their introductions echoed through the school auditorium as they took the stage. The students fell silent with curiosity.

"Good afternoon, students. I'm Dr Mehra," Naureen declared with a warm smile, his

charismatic presence filling the room. "Today, we embark on a journey through history, exploring the abolition of slavery and the unsung heroes who paved the way for a more just world."

Elodie stepped forward, her eyes shining with determination. "Greetings, young minds. I'm Mrs. Laurent, and I believe that understanding our history empowers us to shape a better future. Together, we'll delve into the untold stories that have shaped the world we live in."

Finally, the spotlight turned to Kanchana, who had transformed from a reserved researcher into a dynamic speaker. "Hello, everyone. I'm Miss Desai, and I'm here to bridge the gap between the past and the present. Let's explore the triumphs and struggles of those who fought against the chains of slavery."

The children, seated in anticipation, listened attentively as the historians wove a narrative that transcended time. Naureen, Elodie , and Kanchana spoke in unison, their voices harmonizing like a well-choreographed symphony.

"History is not a mere chronicle of events; it's a living, breathing entity that shapes our present and future," Naureen declared, his resonant voice filling the auditorium. Elodie followed, emphasizing the importance of delving beyond surface-level narratives, urging students to question assumptions and seek the truth. Kanchana, having undergone significant character development in her journey, stood confidently beside her colleagues, embodying a newfound strength and eloquence.

Kanchana, once perceived as reserved, had blossomed into a dynamic speaker, drawing from her experiences to infuse authenticity into their presentations. Her growth exemplified the transformative power of historical exploration, echoing the sentiments of Manisha Sinha's own evolution as a scholar. Kanchana's words, though measured, carried a weight of sincerity and passion that resonated with the audience.

As they spoke, the children, initially quiet, began to murmur amongst themselves. Curiosity sparked in their eyes, and hands shot up eagerly as they were given the opportunity to engage with the historians.

A young voice piped up from the crowd, "What can we do today to make a difference like those abolitionists did back then?"

Naureen, Elodie , and Kanchana exchanged knowing glances before Kanchana responded, "Great question! By learning from history, you're already taking the first step. Listen, empathize, and speak up against injustice. You have the power to shape a world that reflects the values of compassion and equality."

Encouraged by the response, more questions flowed from the engaged audience, creating a vibrant dialogue between the historians and the young minds eager to absorb the lessons of the past.

"Let us remember that the fight against injustice is an ongoing struggle, and we are all custodians of the lessons history imparts," Elodie proclaimed, her gaze unwavering. Kanchana,
drawing on her personal development, emphasized the role of empathy in understanding the nuances of historical narratives. Together, they urged students to be catalysts for change, echoing the spirit of Sinha's call to action.

In unison, Naureen, Elodie , and Kanchana concluded their collective address, leaving an indelible
impression on the young minds before them. Inspired by the legacy of Manisha Sinha, they had not only become modern-day torchbearers but also architects of a more enlightened and just future. The applause that followed was not just for the captivating stories and historical insights but for the shared vision of a world where the echoes of the past inspire a brighter
tomorrow.

The children, now energized and inspired, left the auditorium with a renewed sense of
purpose, ready to carry the torch forward into a future shaped by understanding, empathy, and justice. The historians, observing the ripple effect of their words, smiled at the thought of a
new generation poised. The journey persisted towards a more equitable world.

As the auditorium emptied, a small group of students approached Naureen, Elodie , and Kanchana. Among them, a determined young girl spoke up, "Thank you for showing us that history isn't just about the past. It's about our choices today. We'll make sure to keep the flame alive."

Another said "I want to be a historian like you. I am glad that you had opened our eyes to the realm of our choices." The historians exchanged a proud glance, realizing that they had not only imparted knowledge but had ignited a spark of activism within the hearts of the next

generation.

Trio's Diary:

Dear Diary,

14/2/24

Elodie :
Today was like unlocking a hidden talent as a historian, being the modern Manisha Sinha. Our echoing talks, especially delving into the impactful work on abolitionists, ignited a profound curiosity about the abolition of slavery.

Naureen:
The auditorium became a canvas of reflection on the abolitionist's bravery and the broader history of slavery abolition. The stories we uncovered painted a poignant picture of the struggles and triumphs that shaped our understanding of justice and human rights. Who would have thought that slaves resisted like this? It is just not bourgeois liberalism, isn't it? Anyways, I can't wait for tomorrow. It is going to be really fun going to another school,
   giving a talk on the Anglo Saxons, Normans, and Cnut (not Kahoot btw).

Kanchana:
The legacy of these slaves resonated deeply with us. Our inspirational talk wasn't just a stroll through the past about slaves; it fuelled a collective passion for understanding the

complexities of the abolitionist movement and the future it had made. The expedition of words left us inspired and craving more knowledge about the transformative moments in history that continue to shape our present.

Chapter 7: Legacy of Anglo- Saxons

The trio prepared to address the inquisitive students once again, a wave of excitement filled the auditorium. Naureen, Elodie , and Kanchana stood poised at the front, ready to embark on another journey through the Elodie ls of time.

"Good morning, everyone," Naureen greeted with his trademark warmth, his eyes twinkling with anticipation. "Today, we delve into a fascinating tapestry of history, connecting the threads of Cnut, the Anglo-Saxons, and the Normans."

At the mention of Cnut, a wave of murmurs rippled through the classroom. "OMG, a Kahoot, that's fun!" exclaimed one enthusiastic student.

Naureen chuckled softly, shaking his head. "No, not Kahoot, Cnut," he clarified, drawing amused smiles from his companions and a chorus of understanding from the students.

"Indeed," Elodie interjected, stepping forward to add context to the discussion. "Cnut, or Canute, was a remarkable figure in history, a king who defied the tides of time and left an enduring legacy."

Kanchana, seizing the opportunity to engage the audience, continued, "Cnut's reign marked a

pivotal moment in the transition from the Anglo-Saxon era to the Norman conquest. His story is intertwined with the fabric of English history, illustrating the complexities of power,

succession, and cultural exchange."

As Kanchana spoke, images of Cnut's conquests and his efforts to consolidate power flashed across the screen, captivating the audience, and igniting their curiosity.

"Cnut's rule exemplifies the interconnectedness of historical events," Naureen continued, his voice resonating with passion. "His marriage to Emma of Normandy forged alliances that shaped the course of English history. Through his reign, we see the convergence of Anglo-

Saxon and Norman influences, laying the groundwork for the events that would unfold in the years to come."

The students listened intently as Naureen wove a narrative that connected the dots between past and present, demonstrating how the echoes of history reverberate through the ages.

"From the Anglo-Saxon Chronicles to the Bayeux Tapestry, the story of Cnut and his

successors is immortalized in the Elodie ls of time," Elodie remarked, her gaze sweeping across the room. "By understanding the intricacies of this period, we gain insight into the foundations of modern England and the rich tapestry of cultures that have shaped its identity."

The trio continued to elaborate on the various aspects of Cnut's reign, exploring his diplomatic endeavours, military conquests, and cultural contributions. Through their
engaging presentation, they painted a vivid picture of a pivotal era in English history, sparking curiosity and prompting questions from the captivated audience.

As the class dispersed, a sense of wonder lingered in the air, mingling with the echoes of centuries past. Inspired by the lessons of history, the students departed with a deeper
understanding of the forces that have shaped their world, eager to uncover the hidden truths that lie beneath the surface of time. And as Naureen, Elodie , and Kanchana watched them go, they
knew that their journey had only just begun, for the tapestry of history is vast and ever- unfolding, waiting to be explored by curious minds eager to unravel its mysteries.

Trio's diary:

Dear Diary,

Elodie :
Today was like unlocking a hidden talent as a historian, with us being the world-class

historians. Our echoing talks, especially delving into the impactful work on Anglo Saxons and Cnut, ignited a profound curiosity about the Anglo Saxon England, along with its link to the Normans.

Naureen:
The auditorium became a canvas of reflection on the Saxons' valour and the broader history of England, the fight of religions and the many rulers who shaped Anglo Saxon England. The stories we uncovered painted a significant picture of the struggles and triumphs that shaped our understanding of justice and human rights. Who would have thought that slaves resisted

like this? It is just not bourgeois liberalism, isn't it? Anyways, I can't wait for the next expedition. Who knows what awaits us, am I right?

Kanchana:
The legacy of these Saxons resonated deeply with us. Our inspirational talk wasn't just a stroll through the past about Saxons and Cnut; it fuelled a collective passion for

understanding the complexities of their actions and the future it had made. The expedition of words left us inspired and craving more knowledge about the transformative moments in history that continue to shape our present.

Chapter 8: the confrontation of the mastermind

The air hung heavy with anticipation as Naureen, Elodie , and Kanchana stood before the looming gates of the ancient mansion, the final bastion of their journey to unveil the truths hidden
within the networks of history. With each step forward, the weight of their mission bore down upon them, the gravity of their confrontation with the mastermind surging high in their
minds.

Pushing open the ornate doors, they entered the dimly lit foyer, the soft glow of candlelight casting eerie shadows across the room. A voice, tinged with a sinister edge, echoed through the darkness, welcoming them with a chilling certainty. "Welcome, historians. I've been
expecting you."

Intimidated by the ominous greeting, Naureen, Elodie , and Kanchana pressed on, their resolve unshakeable as they ventured deeper into the heart of the mansion.

The mastermind emerged from the shadows; their identity cloaked in mystery until this pivotal moment. A former colleague, driven by a thirst for power and a warped vision of rewriting history to suit their own agenda.

Engaging in a verbal spar, the historians and the mastermind clashed, each exchange a battle of intellect and will, as they sought to unravel the truth from the web of lies woven around them.

As the confrontation intensified, revelations tumbled forth, each one a piece of the puzzle

falling into place, leading them closer to the heart of the mystery that had eluded them for so long. Through the twists and turns of the labyrinthine corridors, they uncovered secrets that threatened to upend everything they thought they knew, challenging their perceptions of the past and the present.

But in the face of adversity, it was not brute force or cunning alone that carried them through.

It was the unwavering bond of friendship, forged through trials and tribulations, which gave them the strength to persevere.

As the first light of dawn broke through the windows, illuminating the chamber with a soft golden hue, Naureen, Elodie , and Kanchana emerged from the shadows victorious, their mission accomplished and their bond stronger than ever before.

With hearts full of hope and determination, they stepped out into the new day, ready to

continue their journey wherever it may lead, knowing that together, they were unstoppable in their pursuit of truth and justice.

Later, they walked away from the mansion, leaving the darkness behind them, they knew that their victory was not just theirs alone, but a triumph for history itself. For in facing the

mastermind together, they had not only preserved the integrity of the past but had also ensured a brighter future for generations to come. With each echoing footstep resonating

through the ancient halls, a sense of urgency propelled the trio forward, their hearts pounding with a mix of anticipation and apprehension. They knew that the final confrontation awaited them, a culmination of their relentless pursuit of truth.

As they traversed through the labyrinthine corridors, lined with portraits of long-departed figures, and adorned with artifacts from centuries past, the weight of history seemed to press down upon them, urging them onward toward their ultimate destination. The mastermind and their presence shrouded in darkness, awaited them in the heart of the mansion, where

shadows danced, and whispers of forgotten secrets echoed through the air.

With steely determination etched upon their faces, Naureen, Elodie , and Kanchana squared their
shoulders, ready to face whatever challenges lay ahead. For they knew that the fate of history itself hung in the abyss of what awaits next. The verbal sparring between the historians and
the mastermind crackled with intensity, each exchange a test of wit and cunning. But beneath the surface, a battle of ideologies raged, pitting the desire for truth against the allure of power.

With every revelation, the pieces of the puzzle fell into place, unveiling a tapestry of deceit and manipulation that threatened to rewrite the course of history.

Nevertheless, the amidst the chaos and confusion, the bond between Naureen, Elodie , and Kanchana remained unbreakable, a beacon of light amidst the encroaching darkness.

As dawn arose, casting its golden rays upon the scene, a sense of resolution enveloped them. The mastermind's machinations had been thwarted, and the truth had emerged victorious.

Stepping out into the crisp morning air, the trio breathed a collective sigh of relief, their spirits buoyed by their power and intelligence prevailed against all odds.

As they observed the horizon, the sun rising majestically, with hues of orange and pink
painting the sky, they knew that their journey was far from over. For the pursuit of history's secrets was a never-ending quest, one that would continue to inspire and challenge them for years to come.

With newfound resolutions and a renewed sense of purpose, Naureen, Elodie , and Kanchana set forward into the dawn, eager to uncover the next chapter in the ever-unfolding saga of the past. And though the road ahead would surely be fraught with obstacles, they faced it with heads held high and hearts filled with hope, for they knew that together, they were
  unstoppable.

Trio's diary:

Dear Diary,

Naureen: Here was a day I won't soon forget. The weight of our mission pressed heavily upon us as we approached the ancient mansion, but with Elodie and Kanchana by my side, I felt a sense of strength and determination. The confrontation with the mastermind tested our intellect and

resolve, but in the end, our bond proved unbreakable. As we walked away from the darkness behind us, I couldn't help but feel a surge of pride knowing that together, we had preserved

the integrity of history itself.

Elodie : Diary today was a whirlwind of emotions and challenges. The anticipation as we entered the mansion was palpable, but with Naureen and Kanchana beside me, I knew we could face whatever lay ahead. The verbal spar with the mastermind was intense, but our unity and friendship ultimately led us to victory. As we stepped into the dawn, I felt a sense of

accomplishment knowing that our pursuit of truth had prevailed. Our journey continues, but I face the future with optimism and determination, knowing that together, we are unstoppable.

Kanchana: Hello, today was a day filled with twists and turns, both literal and metaphorical. The atmosphere in the mansion was heavy with tension, but with Naureen and Elodie at my side, I felt a sense of solidarity and purpose. The battle of intellect with the mastermind tested our limits, but our unwavering bond saw us through to the end. As we emerged victorious into the dawn, I couldn't help but feel grateful for the friendship that had carried us through. Our journey may be far from over, but with Naureen and Elodie by my side, I know we can face whatever

challenges come our way.

Chapter 9: Secrets of ancient Mayan temples

The dense canopy of the Central American jungle enveloped Naureen, Elodie , and Kanchana as they ventured deeper into the heart of the Mayan territory, where the echoes of an ancient
civilization beckoned with whispers of untold secrets.

Guided by cryptic clues and ancient manuscripts, the trio navigated through the labyrinthine maze of towering trees and tangled vines, their senses alive with anticipation. The humid air was thick with the scent of exotic flowers, and the vibrant calls of tropical birds echoed through the verdant canopy above.

"Keep your eyes peeled, everyone. Who knows what we might stumble upon," Naureen urged, his voice filled with excitement.

As they trekked through the dense foliage, they stumbled upon remnants of Mayan
civilization scattered amidst the undergrowth – weathered stone altars, crumbling pyramids, and intricate carvings adorned with glyphs and symbols.

Amidst the lush greenery, they stumbled upon a hidden grove where chilli peppers and fresh cocoa beans grew in abundance, an unexpected treasure trove amidst the jungle's bounty.

"Looks like we've hit the jackpot!" Elodie exclaimed, her eyes lighting up with excitement.

Eager to experience the flavours of the past, they decided to recreate the spicy cocoa drink that the Mayans had enjoyed centuries ago. Gathering the ingredients, they brewed a potent concoction, blending the fiery heat of chilli peppers with the rich, earthy flavour of cocoa beans.

"Here goes nothing," Naureen said with a grin as he raised his cup to his lips, taking a tentative sip.

The fiery heat of the drink took them by surprise, leaving Elodie and Kanchana spluttering and reaching for their water bottles.

"Whoa, that's spicy!" Kanchana exclaimed, her eyes watering.

Undeterred by the unexpected heat, they continued their journey into the heart of the temple, their determination unyielding as they unravelled the mysteries hidden within its ancient halls.

Entering the temple, they were greeted by the dim flicker of torchlight illuminating the walls adorned with intricate hieroglyphs and bas-reliefs depicting scenes of Mayan life and myth.

"These carvings are incredible," Elodie marvelled, tracing her fingers along the weathered stone.

Amongst the carvings, they discovered references to the cocoa bean – a sacred symbol of abundance and vitality in Mayan culture.

Delving deeper into the temple's labyrinthine passages, they encountered chambers filled with treasures – ornate pottery, jade ornaments, and intricately woven textiles, each a
testament to the wealth and sophistication of Mayan civilization.

"Imagine the stories these artifacts could tell," Kanchana mused, her eyes sparkling with wonder.

But their journey into the heart of the temple was not without peril, as they encountered ancient traps and puzzles designed to confound and ensnare intruders.

"Watch your step, there could be more traps ahead," Naureen warned, his voice echoing through the dim corridors.

Undeterred by the dangers that lay ahead, Naureen, Elodie , and Kanchana pressed on, their
        determination unyielding as they unravelled the mysteries hidden within the temple's walls.

And as they emerged from the depths of the temple, clutching ancient artifacts and newfound knowledge, they couldn't help but marvel at the resilience and ingenuity of the Mayan people, whose legacy continued to echo through the ages.

Reflecting on their journey, they pondered the interconnectedness of history, from the rise and fall of ancient civilizations to the enduring impact of their legacies on the world today.

"This journey has been truly remarkable," Elodie said, her voice filled with awe. "I feel like we've only scratched the surface of what's out there."

And as they prepared to leave the jungle behind and return to the modern world, they carried with them not only artifacts and treasures but also a newfound appreciation for the intricate
tapestry of human history, where every artifact, every symbol, and every story was a thread in the vast and timeless fabric of the past.

Within the heart of the dense jungle, where sunlight filtered through the canopy in dappled patterns, the trio's journey took on a mythical quality. Each step felt like a passage through
time, as if they were walking in the footsteps of the ancient Mayans who once called this land their home.

Along the way, they encountered remnants of Mayan settlements, hidden beneath layers of foliage and tangled roots. These silent witnesses to the past spoke volumes about the ingenuity and resilience of the Mayan people, who thrived in harmony with their environment.

As they delved deeper into the jungle, guided by the cryptic clues they had uncovered, the air hummed with anticipation. They knew they were on the brink of discovering something truly remarkable – the secrets of an ancient temple that had stood the test of time.

The scent of cocoa beans and chilli peppers lingered in the air, carrying with it echoes of a

bygone era when the Mayans revered these precious commodities as more than just culinary delights. To them, cocoa was a sacred gift from the gods, while chilli peppers added a fiery touch to their rituals.

The journey to the temple was not without its challenges. The jungle tested their endurance with its sweltering heat, treacherous terrain, and hidden dangers lurking beneath the verdant canopy. But with each obstacle they overcame, their determination only grew stronger.

Finally, as they emerged from the dense foliage, the temple rose before them like a sentinel of the past, its weathered stone façade bearing witness to centuries of history. It stood as a

testament to the ingenuity and artisanry of the Mayan people, who had built it with nothing but simple tools and unwavering determination.

Stepping across the threshold, they were enveloped by the cool darkness of the temple's

interior. Torch in hand, they ventured deeper into its depths, their senses alert for any sign of the secrets that lay hidden within.

Inside, the walls were adorned with intricate carvings and glyphs, each one a puzzle waiting to be solved. They deciphered the ancient symbols, piecing together a story of gods and

heroes, rituals, and sacrifices, woven into the very fabric of the temple itself.

But as they delved deeper, they encountered more than just carvings on the walls. They

stumbled upon hidden chambers filled with treasures – golden artifacts, jade ornaments, and ceremonial objects crafted with unparalleled skill.

Amongst these treasures, they found evidence of the Mayans' sophisticated trade networks, which extended far beyond the borders of their empire. They learned of the cocoa trade,

which played a central role in the economy of the ancient Mayan world.

The Mayans' mastery of cocoa cultivation and processing techniques allowed them to produce a high-quality product coveted by neighbouring civilizations, including the Aztecs. It was through trade that cocoa beans found their way into the hands of the Aztec empire, where they were revered as a symbol of wealth and power.

As they pieced together the puzzle of the Mayans' relationship with cocoa, they gained a deeper appreciation for the intricate web of connections that linked ancient civilizations across time and space.

And as they emerged from the depths of the temple, their hearts brimming with newfound knowledge and understanding, they knew that their journey had only just begun. For the
secrets they had uncovered were but a glimpse into the vast tapestry of human history, waiting to be explored and understood.

The inspired trio left with a better tomorrow, wondering what awaits next. Yet another exhilarating yet cryptic expedition lays in their hearts.

Trio's Diary:

Dear Diary,

Naureen: Today's journey into the heart of the Mayan territory was nothing short of
extraordinary. The dense jungle, teeming with life, seemed to whisper secrets of a bygone era as we ventured deeper into its depths. The discovery of the ancient temple was a testament to the ingenuity and artisanry of the Mayan people, and delving into its depths filled me with a sense of awe and reverence. Unravelling the mysteries hidden within its walls, especially the significance of cocoa in Mayan culture, was truly enlightening. I can't wait to see where our next expedition takes us.

Elodie : Hey Diary, today's expedition into the Mayan jungle was both exhilarating and
enlightening. The dense canopy of the jungle seemed to hold echoes of ancient whispers as we journeyed deeper into its heart. The discovery of the ancient temple was a breathtaking
moment, and exploring its depths filled me with a sense of wonder. The significance of cocoa in Mayan culture, especially its role in trade and rituals, shed new light on the complexities of ancient civilizations. I feel privileged to have been a part of this expedition and can't wait to see what other secrets history holds.

Kanchana: Diary, today's adventure in the Mayan territory was unlike anything I've experienced before. The dense jungle, with its vibrant colours and cacophony of sounds, felt like stepping into another world. The discovery of the ancient temple was awe-inspiring, and delving into its depths was both thrilling and humbling. Learning about the importance of cocoa in Mayan culture was a revelation, and it made me appreciate the intricacies of ancient civilizations

even more. As we prepare for our next expedition, I feel grateful for the opportunity to

uncover history's secrets alongside Naureen and Elodie , knowing that our journey is far from over.

Chapter 10: secrets of the hidden society:

The cobblestone streets of Renaissance Italy echoed with the whispers of a bygone era as

Naureen, Elodie , and Kanchana embarked on their quest to uncover the secrets of this fabled period in history. The air was alive with the scent of spices from the markets and the melodies of street performers, transporting them back to a time of unparalleled creativity and innovation.

Elodie , with intimate exhilaration, blurred " We are guided by cryptic clues and ancient

manuscripts, the trio navigated the labyrinthine alleys and bustling marketplaces of Florence, where the legacy of the Renaissance was etched into every stone and painted onto every

canvas."

Kanchana interrupted, "Look at the masterpieces of Michelangelo, Leonardo da Vinci, and

Botticelli, each stroke of the brush a testament to the genius of the age. Art and architecture in that era was unreal."

Amidst the splendour of the city's grand palaces and ornate cathedrals, they stumbled upon rumours of a clandestine society of scholars and artists, whose influence extended far beyond the confines of the visible world. Whispers of secret meetings and hidden agendas fuelled their curiosity, driving them deeper into the heart of the mystery.

With hearts pounding with excitement, they delved deeper into the shadows, their senses alive with the thrill of discovery. For they knew that within the hidden society lay the key to unlocking the mysteries of the Renaissance. Their quest became a race against time, as they sought to unravel the secrets before they were lost to the sands of history.

As they infiltrated the society's inner circle, they were met with suspicion and intrigue at every turn. Dark secrets and hidden agendas lurked behind the façade of scholarly pursuits

and artistic endeavours, threatening to unravel the very fabric of their reality. They navigated a world of double-crosses and deceit, never knowing who they could trust.

Yet amidst the intrigue and deception, they uncovered fragments of truth; Clues that pointed to a deeper conspiracy at play, stretched back through the Elodie ls of time. They pieced

together a puzzle of ancient texts and hidden symbols, unravelling a tapestry of lies woven by those who sought to rewrite history for their own gain.

Amongst the society's members, they encountered figures of legend and lore – scholars

steeped in ancient wisdom, artists whose brushstrokes held the power to captivate the soul, and nobles whose wealth and influence shaped the course of history. They walked amongst giants, their footsteps echoing through the corridors of time.

But as they delved deeper into the society's secrets, they realized that not all was as it seemed.

Hidden agendas and rivalries simmered beneath the surface, threatening to tear the society apart from within. They navigated a treacherous world of political intrigue and personal ambition, never knowing who they could trust.

Undeterred by the dangers that lurked in the shadows, Naureen, Elodie
, and Kanchana pressed on, their determination unyielding as they
unravelled the mysteries hidden within the society's
hallowed halls. They faced countless obstacles and challenges, each
one testing their resolve and pushing them to their limits.

With each revelation, they pieced together a tapestry of intrigue and
betrayal, uncovering a conspiracy that spanned centuries and reached
to the highest echelons of power. They
uncovered secrets that had been buried for centuries, shining a light
into the darkest corners of history.

And as they emerged from the shadows, clutching ancient manuscripts
and priceless artifacts, they knew that their journey had only just
begun. For the secrets of the Renaissance were vast and multifaceted,
waiting to be explored and understood by those braves enough to seek
them out. They vowed to continue their quest, knowing that the truth
was worth any sacrifice.

With hearts full of hope and determination, they set forth into the
dawn, ready to continue their quest for truth and enlightenment. For
in the shadows of history, where secrets lurked

and mysteries abounded, they knew that they were destined for greatness. Their journey was far from over, but they faced the future with courage and conviction, knowing that they carried with them the knowledge of the ages.

Despite the allure of the Renaissance's artistic splendour, they remained vigilant, knowing that danger lurked around every corner. They encountered shadowy figures in darkened
alleyways and cryptic messages hidden within the pages of ancient tomes, each one a clue leading them closer to the truth.

Naureen stated, " We must delve deeper into the hidden society, they uncovered evidence of forbidden knowledge and arcane rituals, hinting at a darker side to the Renaissance's
intellectual enlightenment."

They realized that the pursuit of knowledge came with a price, and that some secrets were best left undisturbed.

Alongside their quest for truth, they grappled with personal challenges and internal conflicts, each member of the trio facing their own demons and doubts. Yet through their shared
determination and unwavering bond, they found the strength to persevere in the face of adversity.

The deeper they delved into the mysteries of the Renaissance, the more they came to realize

that the past held echoes of the present, and that the struggles of bygone eras still resonated in the modern world. They saw parallels between the political intrigues of the past and the

power struggles of contemporary society, prompting them to reflect on the cyclical nature of history.

And as they emerged from their journey, battered but unbowed, they carried with them not only the artifacts and knowledge they had uncovered, but also a newfound understanding of the complexities of human nature and the enduring power of the human spirit. They knew

that their quest for truth would continue, fuelled by the fire of curiosity and the desire to illuminate the shadows of history.

Trio's diary:

Dear Diary,

Naureen: Salve! Today's exploration of Renaissance Italy was nothing short of captivating. The cobblestone streets of Florence whispered tales of a bygone era, and every corner held the
promise of discovery. The clandestine society we encountered added an air of mystery to our journey, and uncovering their secrets was both thrilling and challenging. Despite the dangers we faced, I feel invigorated by our quest for knowledge and truth. The parallels we
discovered between the past and the present have left me with a deeper appreciation for the complexities of history. I can't wait to continue our journey and see where it leads us next.

Elodie : Ciao! Today's journey through Renaissance Italy was a whirlwind of excitement and intrigue. The beauty of Florence's architecture and artistry was matched only by the secrets we uncovered within the hidden society. Navigating the treacherous world of political
intrigue and personal ambition tested our resolve, but our bond as a trio remained
unbreakable. As we emerge from this adventure, I feel a sense of fulfilment knowing that our quest for truth has only just begun. The lessons we've learned about the cyclical nature of
history have left me with a newfound appreciation for the complexities of the human experience.

Kanchana: Come estai! Our expedition into Renaissance Italy was like stepping into a world of wonder and mystery. The streets of Florence were alive with the echoes of history, and every alleyway held the promise of adventure. Uncovering the secrets of the clandestine society
was both exhilarating and unnerving, but with Naureen and Elodie by my side, I felt a sense of

confidence and determination. As we reflect on our journey, I am filled with gratitude for the opportunity to explore the depths of history and uncover its hidden truths. Our quest may be far from over, but I face the future with optimism and excitement, knowing that together, we are unstoppable.

Chapter 11: lost in the Amazon.

The dense, humid air of the Amazon rainforest enveloped Naureen, Elodie , and Kanchana as they ventured into the heart of one of the world's most treacherous environments. The cacophony of wildlife sounds surrounded them, a stark contrast to the urban landscapes they had navigated before. It felt as if they had stepped into another world entirely, where the rules of civilization no longer applied, and nature reigned supreme.

Guided by fragmented journals and faded maps, the trio embarked on their expedition to uncover the truth behind the mysterious disappearance of a 19th-century expedition. Rumours of forgotten cities and hidden treasures fuelled their determination, driving them deeper into the uncharted wilderness. They knew the risks they faced – deadly predators, unforgiving terrain, and the ever-present threat of disease – but they were undeterred, their resolve steeling them against the dangers that lay ahead.

As they hacked their way through the dense undergrowth, they encountered obstacles at every turn – impassable rivers, venomous creatures, and towering trees that seemed to reach for the sky. Each step brought them closer to danger, yet they pressed on, fuelled by their thirst for discovery. The relentless humidity weighed heavy on their bodies, and the incessant buzzing of insects filled their ears, but still, they forged ahead, driven by a sense of purpose that burned bright within them.

Along the way, they uncovered traces of the lost expedition, rusted machetes, tattered clothing, and faded campfires, silent reminders of the perils that awaited them. Yet amidst the wreckage, they also found clues that hinted at a greater mystery – symbols carved into trees, cryptic messages scrawled in journals. Each discovery fuelled their determination, spurring them onward in their quest for answers.

With fear, Naureen trembled, "I don't know how we are going to make it. We are literally stuck at the abyss of our life, with barely any human contact."

Kanchana interrupted with the utmost fear and intrigue, "it seems there are plenty of pineapples and cocoa beans."

Scanning through the forest floor, Elodie stated, "the water seems to be abundant nevertheless, we are unaware of what happens when it is drunk."

Despite the dangers that surrounded them, they remained undeterred, knowing that the answers they sought lay hidden within the heart of the jungle. They navigated a world of shifting alliances and hidden dangers, never knowing who, or what, they could trust. They forged alliances with Indigenous tribes, learning from their ancient wisdom and gaining invaluable insights into the secrets of the rainforest.

As they delved deeper into the wilderness, they encountered Indigenous tribes whose ancient knowledge of the rainforest proved invaluable in their quest. They forged alliances with the tribespeople, exchanging stories and sharing knowledge in a mutual quest for understanding. Together, they braved the dangers of the jungle, their bond growing stronger with each passing day.

Yet the jungle held more than just natural dangers – it also concealed secrets of its own. Strange phenomena and unexplained occurrences tested their resolve, pushing them to their limits as they struggled to make sense of the mysteries that surrounded them. They encountered strange ruins hidden deep within the jungle, remnants of civilizations long forgotten, and encountered creatures that seemed to belong to another world entirely.

But amidst the chaos and uncertainty, they found moments of awe and wonder – breathtaking sunsets, cascading waterfalls, and rare glimpses of elusive wildlife. These fleeting moments of beauty reminded them of the true essence of the rainforest, a delicate balance of life and death. They marvelled at the intricate ecosystems that existed within its depths, each one a testament to the resilience of nature.

As they journeyed deeper into the heart of the jungle, they uncovered the truth behind the lost expedition – a tale of greed and betrayal, of hubris and folly.

With pride, Elodie sighed, "We had pieced together the events that had led to the expedition's demise, unravelling a tapestry of lies woven by those who sought to exploit the riches of the rainforest. We have uncovered hidden cities, lost to the ravages of time, and encountered artifacts that spoke of a civilization long vanished from the earth. Naureen Mehra, Kanchana Desai, we are the historians of hidden truths. The world must see this!"

And as they emerged from the wilderness, battered but unbowed, they carried with them not only the answers they had sought but also a newfound appreciation for the fragile beauty of the Amazon rainforest. They knew that their journey had changed them forever, shaping their understanding of the world and their place within it. They vowed to continue their quest, knowing that the mysteries of the rainforest were far from over.

With hearts full of gratitude and reverence, they bid farewell to the untamed wilderness that had tested them in ways they never could have imagined. Yet they knew that their quest for knowledge would continue, fuelled by the spirit of exploration and the eternal quest for truth. For in the vast expanse of the Amazon rainforest, where danger lurked in every shadow, they had found not only answers but also a sense of purpose that would guide them on their journey for years to come.

As they made their way back to civilization, they reflected on the lessons they had learned during their time in the jungle. They had faced unimaginable challenges and encountered wonders beyond their wildest dreams, but through it all, they had persevered. They knew that they would carry the memories of their expedition with them for the rest of their lives, a testament to the indomitable spirit of human exploration.

And as they returned to the world they had left behind; they knew that they were forever changed by their experiences in the Amazon rainforest. They had glimpsed the true power and majesty of nature, and they vowed to do everything in their power to protect it for future generations. For in the end, they knew that the greatest treasure of all was not gold or jewels, but the beauty and wonder of the natural world.

With a renewed sense of purpose and determination, they set their sights on new horizons, knowing that their journey was far from over. For in the vast expanse of the world, where mysteries awaited and adventures beckoned, they knew that they would always be explorers at heart. And as they disappeared into the distance, their laughter echoing through the jungle, they left behind a legacy of courage and discovery that would inspire generations to come closer and closer.

Trio's diary:

Dear Diary,

    Elodie : We're lost in the Amazon, and every direction looks the same. The canopy above us is so dense that it blocks out most of the sunlight, casting everything in an eerie green light.

    We've been trekking for days, and our supplies are running low. But today, we made an incredible discovery that makes all the hardships worth it. We stumbled upon an ancient, hidden temple, its stone walls covered in intricate carvings and symbols. This is something the world needs to see. It could rewrite history as we know it. Despite our exhaustion and fear, excitement is coursing through me. We have to document this and find our way back to civilization to share it with the world.

Liv: The Amazon is a labyrinth, and we're hopelessly lost. The sounds of the jungle are constant and unnerving—every rustle and chirp could mean danger. But today, amidst our struggle, we found something extraordinary. An ancient temple, overgrown with vines and moss, hidden from the world for who knows how long. The carvings on the walls depict

scenes of a civilization we've never seen before. It's a discovery that could change everything we know about the history of this region. I'm scared and tired, but also exhilarated. We have to survive and get this information out. This temple is too important to be lost again.

Naureen: We're deep in the Amazon and completely lost. The jungle is an unforgiving place, and every step feels like it could be our last. But today, our despair turned to astonishment. We found an ancient temple hidden in the heart of the jungle. The carvings and artifacts inside are unlike anything we've seen before. This discovery is monumental—it could provide

insights into an unknown civilization and their way of life. We're exhausted and on edge, but we must press on. The world needs to know about this temple. It's a beacon of hope and knowledge amidst our struggles. We must find our way out and share this incredible find with the world.

Chapter 12: The Industrial Odyssey:

As the trio ventured through the bustling streets of a rapidly industrializing city, the clamour of machinery and the acrid scent of smoke filled the air. Naureen, Elodie , and Kanchana were on a new mission, disguised as workers in a factory, their true identities concealed as they delved into the heart of the Industrial Revolution.

"This place is unlike anything I've ever seen," Kanchana remarked, her voice barely audibles over the cacophony of whirring gears and clanging metal.

"Indeed, it's a testament to the ingenuity of mankind," Elodie replied, her eyes scanning the rows of steam-powered machines with fascination.

Their journey had brought them to the epicentre of industrial progress, where factories churned out goods at an unprecedented pace, fuelled by the relentless march of progress and the pursuit of profit.

"Remember, we're here to observe and document, not to interfere," Naureen reminded them, his voice tinged with urgency.

As they blended in with the workers, they marvelled at the efficiency of the machines and the sheer scale of production. Yet amidst the hustle and bustle, they couldn't help but notice the toll it took on the workers – the long hours, the dangerous working conditions, and the meagre wages.

"This laissez-faire approach to industry may have its benefits, but at what cost?" Elodie pondered; her brow furrowed with concern.

"Indeed, it seems that human lives are deemed expendable in the pursuit of profit," Kanchana added, her voice filled with indignation.

As they delved deeper into the workings of the factory, they uncovered the evolution of historical appliances and labour practices – from the invention of steam engines to the mechanization of production processes.

"This machine here represents a significant leap forward in industrial efficiency," Naureen observed, pointing to a towering contraption that loomed over the factory floor.

"But at what price?" Kanchana countered, her gaze lingering on the exhausted faces of the workers as they toiled away under its relentless whir.

Their time in the factory opened their eyes to the stark realities of the Industrial Revolution – the stark divide between the haves and have-nots, the exploitation of labour for the sake of progress, and the unchecked power of industrialists driven by the pursuit of profit.

"We must ensure that progress does not come at the expense of human dignity," Elodie declared, her voice resolute with determination.

As they left the factory behind, their minds filled with newfound knowledge and understanding, they knew that their mission was far from over. For the lessons they had learned in the crucible of industry would shape their understanding of history and humanity for years to come.

"And so, our journey continues, into the heart of the past and the soul of mankind," Naureen said, his voice echoing with the weight of their discoveries.

With each step they took, they carried with them the lessons of the Industrial Revolution – a cautionary tale of progress and its pitfalls, a reminder of the importance of compassion and empathy in the face of change.

And as they ventured into the unknown, their resolve unshaken by the challenges that lay ahead, they knew that their journey as undercover historians had only just begun.

Trio's diary:

Dear Diary,

Kanchana: Dear Diary, today's journey into the heart of Andover's industrial landscape was a whirlwind of awe and dismay. The deafening roar of machinery and the acrid scent of smoke filled the air, painting a picture of progress tinged with hardship. As we ventured deeper into the factory, I could not shake the feeling of unease at the exploitation of labour for the sake of progress. The laissez-faire approach to industry may have its merits, but witnessing the toll it takes on the workers was a stark reminder of the injustices of the past. Yet, amidst the adversity, I find solace in our mission to uncover history's truths and advocate for change. With each revelation, I am filled with a sense of determination to make a difference in the world.

Naureen: Today's reflections: our journey into Andover's industrial heartland revealed both the marvels and miseries of the Industrial Revolution. The sprawling factories and deafening machinery painted a picture of progress, but beneath the surface lay the harsh realities faced by the working class. The laissez-faire approach to industry, while driving economic growth, came at a cost – the exploitation of labour and the degradation of human dignity. Our mission to shed light on these injustices has never been more vital. With each revelation, I am reminded of our duty to advocate for change and stand in solidarity with the oppressed.

Elodie : Journal Entry - Today's exploration of Andover's industrial landscape was a poignant reminder of the complexities of progress. The bustling factories and towering smokestacks stood as symbols of innovation, yet the plight of the workers revealed the dark underbelly of industrialization. The laissez-faire approach to industry may have fuelled economic growth, but it came at the expense of human lives and dignity. Our mission to uncover the truths of history and advocate for reform has never been more urgent. With each discovery, I am filled with a renewed sense of purpose and determination to create a better future for all.

Chapter 13: Shadows of Progress

In the heart of Andover, where smokestacks towered like sentinels of progress, Naureen, Elodie , and Kanchana found themselves thrust into the midst of the Industrial Revolution, where the relentless pursuit of innovation drove the wheels of industry ever forward.

"This is where the future is forged," Kanchana remarked, her voice barely audibles over the deafening roar of the factory floor.

"It's a sight to behold," Elodie agreed, her eyes wide with wonder as she took in the sprawling complex of factories and warehouses that stretched as far as the eye could see.

Their mission had brought them to the epicentre of industrial progress, where the promise of prosperity hung in the air like a tangible presence.

"Let's keep a low profile. We don't want to attract any unwanted attention," Naureen cautioned, his eyes scanning the bustling factory floor for any sign of trouble.

As they mingled with the workers, they couldn't help but marvel at the sheer scale of production and the efficiency of the machines. Yet amidst the hustle and bustle, they glimpsed the shadows of exploitation and inequality that lurked in the corners of the factory floor.

"The cost of progress should not be borne on the backs of the working class," Elodie remarked, her voice filled with conviction as she observed the weary faces of the workers.

"Agreed. We must strive for a future where progress benefits all, not just a privileged few," Kanchana added, her eyes flashing with determination.

As they delved deeper into the workings of the factory, they uncovered the dark underbelly of industrialization – the long hours, the dangerous working conditions, and the meagre wages that kept the wheels of progress turning at the expense of human lives.

"This laissez-faire approach to industry is untenable. We must advocate for reforms that prioritize the well-being of workers," Naureen declared, his voice echoing through the cavernous halls of the factory.

Their time in the factory opened their eyes to the harsh realities of progress – the sacrifices made in the name of innovation, and the need for compassion and empathy in the face of change.

"And so, our journey continues, into the heart of progress and the shadows it casts," Elodie said, her voice filled with resolve as they left the factory behind.

With each step they took, they carried with them the lessons of the Industrial Revolution – a reminder of the importance of empathy and solidarity in the face of adversity, and the power of collective action to shape the course of history.

And as they ventured into the unknown, their spirits undaunted by the challenges that lay ahead, they knew that their journey as undercover historians had only just begun.

Trio's diary:

Dear Diary,

Kanchana: Dear Diary, today's journey into the shadows of progress unveiled the harsh realities of the Industrial Revolution. The sprawling factories of Andover may have heralded a new era, but beneath the surface lay the stark divide between privilege and poverty. The laissez-faire approach to industry may have fuelled economic growth, but at what cost to the working class? Our mission to advocate for reform and human dignity has never been more vital. With each revelation, I am filled with a sense of urgency and determination to make a difference in the world.

Naureen: Today's reflections: our exploration of Andover's industrial landscape brought to light the injustices faced by the working class. The relentless pursuit of progress may have transformed the city, but it came at a steep cost to human lives. The laissez-faire approach to industry, while fostering economic growth, perpetuated inequality, and exploitation. Our mission to challenge these injustices and advocate for change has never been more urgent. With each revelation, I am reminded of the power of solidarity and collective action in the face of adversity.

Elodie : Journal Entry - Today's expedition into the shadows of progress revealed the harsh realities of the Industrial Revolution. The sprawling factories and crowded tenements painted a grim picture of life in the industrial age. The laissez-faire approach to industry, while driving economic growth, came at the expense of human dignity and well-being. Our mission to shine a light on these injustices and advocate for reform has never been more crucial. With each discovery, I am filled with a renewed sense of purpose and determination to create a more just and equitable society.

Chapter 14: Beneath the Surface

The fog settled thick and heavy around the Andover Workhouse as Elodie , Naureen, and Kanchana approached under the cover of darkness. Their hearts pounded with a mix of fear and excitement. Dressed in rags to blend in, they had one goal: uncover the grim realities hidden behind the workhouse's walls. The grim facade loomed over them, a dark silhouette against the moonlit sky.

Elodie , the determined leader of the trio, signalled for them to stop just before they reached the main gate. "Remember," she whispered, "we're just here to observe and gather information.

Stay close and stay quiet."

Naureen nodded; his face set in a determined frown. He adjusted the cap that concealed his blond hair. Kanchana, the youngest and most agile, glanced around nervously, her eyes wide with anticipation.

They slipped through a gap in the fence, their breath visible in the cold night air. The workhouse yard was eerily silent, except for the occasional cough or groan from inside the building. The stench of decay and human suffering assaulted their senses.

Inside the main hall, they saw rows of filthy beds filled with emaciated figures. The sight was worse than any of them had imagined. Men, women, and children lay huddled together, their eyes hollow and devoid of hope. Elodie clenched her fists, her heart aching for the souls trapped in this place.

"Keep moving," Naureen urged, his voice barely audible. They needed to find a way to document what they saw without drawing attention to themselves.

They made their way to the infirmary, where the true extent of the workhouse's horrors became evident. People lay on straw mats, their bodies ravaged by disease and malnutrition. Kanchana, struggling to maintain her composure, pulled out a small notebook and began to sketch the scene, capturing the gaunt faces and skeletal limbs with heartbreaking accuracy.

A groan from a nearby bed caught their attention. A man, barely conscious, reached out a trembling hand. "Water... please..."

Elodie hurried to his side, producing a small flask from beneath her cloak. As she helped him drink, she noticed the sores on his skin, the feverish glaze in his eyes. "How long have you been here?" she asked softly.

"Too long," he rasped. "They don't care about us. We're just bodies to fill the space."

Naureen and Kanchana exchanged a grim look. They had to get this information out, but they also needed to find a way to help these people. The man's words hung heavy in the air as they continued their covert investigation.

Their next stop was the kitchen, where they found a thin, watery gruel being prepared. The smell was revolting, and it was clear that this meagre fare was all the inhabitants received. Kanchana sketched quickly, her hands shaking with anger.

Suddenly, the door creaked open, and the trio froze. A stern-looking matron entered, her eyes scanning the room suspiciously. Elodie motioned for Naureen and Kanchana to hide behind a stack of crates.

The matron began to ladle out the gruel, muttering to herself about the "ungrateful wretches" under her care. Elodie 's blood boiled, but she remained still, knowing that their mission depended on not being discovered.

When the matron finally left, they slipped out of their hiding place and made their way to the children's ward. Here, the air was thick with the sound of coughing and whimpering. The children, many of them orphaned or abandoned, lay in filthy cots. Their eyes, once full of life, were now dull and lifeless.

Kanchana's tears flowed freely as she sketched, each stroke of her pencil a silent testament to the cruelty they witnessed. Naureen took detailed notes, his face a mask of determination.

Elodie knelt beside a little girl whose cheeks were sunken, her tiny frame shivering under a thin blanket. "We'll find a way to help you," Elodie whispered, her voice breaking. "I promise."

As dawn approached, the trio knew they had to leave before the workhouse staff discovered their presence. They retraced their steps, slipping back through the gap in the fence just as the first rays of sunlight pierced the morning fog.

Back in their hideout, they reviewed the sketches and notes, the weight of what they had seen pressing heavily on them. "We need to expose this," Elodie said, her voice fierce with resolve. "The world has to know what's happening here."

Naureen nodded, with sadness enveloping him. "We need to find a way to get these people out. They can't survive much longer in those conditions."

Kanchana wiped her eyes, her expression one of steely determination. "We'll do it. We have to."

As they planned their next steps, the memory of the haunted faces they had seen in the workhouse fuelled their resolve. They were not just historians anymore; they were witnesses to an atrocity, and they would stop at nothing to bring justice to the forgotten souls of the Andover Workhouse.

Trio's Diary:

Dear Diary,

Elodie : Tonight, we infiltrated the Andover Workhouse. The conditions are worse than we feared. The people are suffering immensely—starvation, disease, and neglect are rampant. I feel both anger and sorrow for what we've witnessed. Seeing the hollow eyes and skeletal frames of the inmates was almost unbearable. The smell of decay and sickness still lingers in my nostrils. It's clear that the people here are treated as less than human. We must expose this atrocity and find a way to help them. This is no place for anyone to live, and we can't let their suffering go unnoticed. I can't stop thinking about the man who reached out for water. His desperation and hopelessness haunt me. We need to act quickly, or more lives will be lost to this inhumanity.

Liv: The children's ward broke my heart. Their eyes, once filled with innocence, are now empty. Sketching their plight was the hardest thing I've ever done. Each child looked more fragile and lost than the next. They're not just numbers or statistics—they're little souls with dreams and hopes that have been shattered. I felt so helpless watching them shiver under thin blankets, hearing their weak coughs. We have to do something to save them. They deserve better than this nightmare. Their suffering is a stain on humanity that we need to erase. I can't shake the image of the tiny girl with sunken cheeks. I promised her we'd help, and we have to keep that promise. These children deserve a chance at life, not a slow death in this prison of misery.

Naureen: We saw humanity at its lowest tonight. The workhouse is a place of despair and death. Taking notes felt almost futile against the overwhelming horror, but we need this evidence to fight back. The sight of the emaciated bodies and the sound of desperate pleas for help will haunt me forever. Every corner we turned revealed more neglect and abuse. We have to make sure the world knows the truth. No one should live like this. It's up to us to be their voice and to bring about the change that can save them. This mission has become more than just an investigation; it's a call to action. I can't get the image of the thin, watery gruel out of my mind. It's not fit for animals, let alone humans. We're not just documenting history anymore—we're part of it, and we have to make sure this dark chapter ends with hope and justice for those trapped inside.

Chapter 15: The Mastermind Strikes Again

"Kanchana, are you sure this is the right decision?" Naureen, with a perplexed yet anticipated facial expression, asked as they stood at the entrance of the dimly lit café.

Kanchana nodded resolutely, her eyes scanning the interior for a familiar face. "We need him, Naureen. If anyone can help us crack this case, it's Daniel."

Naureen sighed, running a hand through his tousled hair. "I just hope we can trust him after everything."

Before Kanchana could respond, Elodie , the ever-curious historian, and their closest friend,

appeared behind them, her eyes twinkling with curiosity. "Are we going in or what? I've been dying to see Daniel again."

The trio entered the café, the rich aroma of coffee and baked goods enveloping them. They spotted Daniel Reeve at a corner table, his sharp eyes already fixed on them. He looked older, more worn, but there was still that same spark of intelligence and cunning in his gaze.

"Kanchana, Naureen, Elodie ," Daniel greeted them with a faint smile, standing up to shake their hands. "It's been a long time."

"Too long," Kanchana replied, taking a seat opposite him. Naureen and Elodie followed suit, a tense silence settling over them.

"So, what brings you to seek out an old colleague like me?" Daniel asked, his eyes flickering with curiosity.

"We're working on a case," Naureen began, leaning forward. "A series of robberies, but they're... unique."

"Unique how?" Daniel's interest was piqued.

Elodie pulled out a folder from her bag and handed it to Daniel. "These robberies have all the hallmarks of someone we've encountered before. Someone who plans meticulously and leaves no trace."

Daniel's eyes scanned the documents, his expression growing more serious by the second. "You're thinking it's The Mastermind."

"We're sure of it," Kanchana said, her voice steady. "And we need your help to catch them."

Daniel leaned back in his chair, a thoughtful look on his face. "It's not going to be easy. The Mastermind is called that for a reason. But I'll help you. On one condition."

"Name it," Naureen said, his eyes narrowing slightly.

"I want a clean slate," Daniel replied. "Help me clear my name from the past... mistakes I've made."

Kanchana glanced at Naureen and Elodie before nodding. "Agreed. We help you; you help us." Daniel's lips curled into a smile. "Then let's get to work."

Hours later, after detailed discussions and pouring over evidence, the group took a break. Naureen and Daniel found themselves alone at the table while Elodie and Kanchana stepped outside for some fresh air.

"How've you been, Daniel?" Naureen asked, breaking the silence. "Really."

Daniel sighed, rubbing his temples. "It's been rough, Naureen. Leaving the force wasn't easy, and I've had to fight my own battles. But this," he gestured to the files on the table, "this is what I miss. The thrill of the chase."

"We missed you too," Naureen admitted. "Despite everything, you were one of the best."

"I made mistakes, Naureen. I let my ambition get the better of me," Daniel said, a note of regret in his voice.

"We all make mistakes," Naureen replied. "It's what you do after that counts."

Outside, Kanchana and Elodie leaned against the café's wall, watching the bustling street. "You think this will work?" Elodie asked, glancing at Kanchana.

"I hope so," Kanchana replied. "We need Daniel's expertise, and he needs a chance to redeem himself. Maybe this case is the key to both."

Elodie nodded thoughtfully. "It's strange seeing him again. Like a ghost from the past."

"Yeah," Kanchana said, her eyes distant. "But sometimes, you need to confront the past to move forward."

Back inside, the group reconvened, their determination renewed.

"Alright," Daniel said, looking each of them in the eye. "We know The Mastermind's pattern. Now we need to predict their next move. We'll need to be one step ahead at all times."

"Any ideas where to start?" Elodie asked.

Daniel nodded, tapping the folder. "We start by revisiting the sites of the previous robberies. There's always something left behind a clue we might have missed."

Kanchana stood up; her expression was resolute. "Then let's get going. The Mastermind isn't going to wait for us."

As they left the café, a sense of purpose united them. The past was behind them, and ahead lay a new challenge – one that they would face together.

Trio's Diary:

Dear Diary,

Kanchana:

Today was a day of confronting old ghosts and making tough decisions. Naureen and I stood at the entrance of the dimly lit café; our minds weighed down by the uncertainty of seeking out Daniel Reeve. But we needed him. The Mastermind's recent string of robberies has us stumped, and if anyone can help us crack this case, it's Daniel. Despite our past, we extended a hand to him, hoping he'd take it. The air in the café was thick with memories and unresolved tension, but we made a pact: we'll help clear Daniel's name if he helps us catch The Mastermind. It's a risky alliance, but sometimes, risks are necessary.

Naureen:

Seeing Daniel again after all these years was surreal. The café, with its cozy atmosphere, seemed an unlikely place for such a reunion. Yet, there we were, discussing the intricacies of a case that only someone of Daniel's calibre could help solve. His condition for helping us—a clean slate— made me uneasy. We've all got our pasts, but Daniel's mistakes still linger. However, the look in his eyes, that spark of determination, reminded me why we once trusted him. As we delved into the case, it felt like old times, despite the shadows of the past. I just hope we can navigate this partnership without reopening old wounds.

Elodie :

The day was filled with a mixture of anticipation and nostalgia. Seeing Daniel again was like meeting a ghost from our past. I couldn't help but feel a pang of curiosity and a bit of hope. The Mastermind's pattern has been elusive, and Daniel's expertise could be the key to solving this. As we discussed the case in the café, I felt a renewed sense of purpose. Outside, Kanchana and I shared a quiet moment, pondering the twists of fate that brought us here. It's strange, yet there's a sense of rightness in facing the past to move forward. Together, we've embarked on this new challenge, and I believe we can overcome it.

Chapter 16: Shadows of the Past

Kanchana Desai, Elodie Laurent, and Naureen Mehra walked back from the cafe in comfortable silence, their minds still buzzing from the unexpected encounter with Daniel Reeve. The meeting had been a mixture of nostalgia and tension, the air heavy with unresolved issues and lingering questions.

As they strolled through the narrow, cobblestone streets of the historic district, the fading afternoon sun cast long shadows, lending an almost ethereal quality to the ancient buildings around them. Kanchana, always the most perceptive of the trio, broke the silence first.

"I never thought we'd see Daniel again," she said, her voice barely above a whisper. "Not after everything that happened."

Elodie , her face partially obscured by a cascade of dark curls, nodded thoughtfully. "He's changed. There's a darkness in his eyes that wasn't there before."

Naureen, ever the pragmatist, shrugged. "People change, Elodie . We all have. But that doesn't mean we can't still reach him."

They continued their walk, the atmosphere gradually shifting from the awkwardness of their earlier encounter to a more reflective tone. The trio found themselves at the entrance of their shared workspace, a converted Victorian house that served as their research headquarters.

They stepped inside, the familiar scent of old books and polished wood welcoming them.

The large, oak-panelled study room was their sanctuary, filled with shelves of ancient tomes, maps, and artifacts. Kanchana settled into her favourite armchair, a plush, deep-red antique that had seen better days. Elodie and Naureen took their usual seats across from her, and for a moment, they simply absorbed the comforting familiarity of their surroundings.

Elodie broke the silence, her voice gentle yet probing. "What do you think Daniel's been up to all these years? He mentioned something about a 'great discovery.'"

Kanchana leaned forward; her eyes bright with curiosity. "I think he's been chasing something big. Remember that project we all worked on before... before everything fell apart?"

"The Lost Chronicles," Naureen said, his voice tinged with excitement. "Of course. That was his passion. But we never could quite piece it all together."

Kanchana nodded. "Exactly. But what if he found something? Something that changes everything we thought we knew about history."

Elodie looked sceptical. "But why didn't he come to us sooner? Why now?"

Naureen rubbed his chin thoughtfully. "Maybe he needed time. Or maybe he wanted to be sure before he brought us back into it."

Kanchana glanced at the ornate clock on the mantelpiece, its hands frozen at a quarter past three, a relic of a bygone era. "Whatever his reasons, we need to be prepared. If Daniel's discovery is as significant as he hinted, it could have far-reaching implications."

Elodie sighed, her eyes reflecting a mix of hope and trepidation. "I just hope we can trust him again."

Naureen leaned back; his expression resolute. "We'll have to. If we're going to help him, we need to put the past behind us and focus on the task at hand."

The three historians sat in contemplative silence, each lost in their thoughts. The weight of their shared history hung in the air, but so did the potential for a new beginning.

The next morning, the trio gathered around a large, mahogany table in the centre of the study room. The table was strewn with maps, manuscripts, and various historical artifacts. Kanchana, ever the organized one, had set up a large whiteboard with notes and diagrams detailing their next steps.

"Alright," she began, her voice firm and confident. "We need to start by revisiting our old research on the Lost Chronicles. We might find clues that could help us understand what Daniel has discovered."

Elodie nodded, flipping through a stack of old journals. "I've been thinking about the last fragment we found. Remember how it mentioned a hidden location, 'where the sun meets the earth'?"

Naureen frowned. "Yes, but we never could decipher its exact meaning. It was too cryptic."

Kanchana tapped her pen against the whiteboard. "Maybe we were looking at it the wrong way. What if it's a metaphor, not a literal place?"

Elodie 's eyes lit up. "Like a reference to an ancient myth or a significant historical event?"

"Exactly," Kanchana said, smiling. "We need to think outside the box. Look for patterns in myths, legends, and historical records that fit that description."

Naureen stood up, pacing around the room. "I'll start cross-referencing ancient texts and geographical records. There might be something we've missed."

Kanchana and Elodie nodded, each diving into their respective tasks. Hours passed in a flurry of activity, the room filled with the soft rustle of pages and the occasional exclamation of discovery.

By evening, they reconvened, their excitement palpable. Naureen was the first to speak, holding up an old, weathered map.

"I think I found something," he said, his voice brimming with anticipation. "There's a region in the Middle East, near the ancient city of Ur, which was historically referred to as 'the place where the sun meets the earth.' It's a long shot, but it fits the description."

Kanchana's eyes widened. "That makes sense. Ur was a significant centre of ancient civilization. If the Lost Chronicles were hidden there, it would be a place of great historical importance."

Elodie added, "And it aligns with some of the myths we've studied. Many ancient cultures believed that divine knowledge was hidden in such places."

Kanchana nodded, her mind racing. "We need to verify this. If Daniel is onto something, this could be the breakthrough we've been waiting for."

Naureen grinned. "Looks like we're going to Ur."

The next few days were a whirlwind of preparations. Kanchana, Elodie , and Naureen worked tirelessly, gathering the necessary resources for their expedition. They reached out to contacts in the archaeological community, secured permits, and arranged for travel.

Finally, the day arrived. They stood at the entrance of their headquarters, bags packed and ready for the journey ahead. Kanchana looked at her friends, her heart swelling with a mix of pride and excitement.

"This is it," she said, her voice steady. "We're going to uncover the truth, no Naureener what it takes."

Elodie smiled, her eyes shining with determination. "For history." Naureen nodded; his expression resolute. "And for Daniel."

With that, they set off, the weight of the past lifting as they embraced the promise of a new adventure. Together, they would face the unknown, driven by their shared passion for history and their unwavering bond.

As they disappeared into the bustling streets, the shadows of the past gave way to the bright light of possibility, illuminating their path forward.

Trio's diary:

Dear Diary, Naureen:

Today was like stepping back into the past and confronting old wounds. Walking back from the café with Kanchana and Elodie , I couldn't shake the feeling of tension mixed with nostalgia. Seeing Daniel again after all these years was surreal. He's different—there's a darkness in his eyes that wasn't there before. Yet, there's still that spark of intelligence we once admired. The meeting was intense, but we made a pact: we'll help clear his name if he helps us catch The Mastermind. It's a risky alliance, but it's one we need to take. Tomorrow, we're diving back into our research on the Lost Chronicles. Feels like old times.

Elodie :

The encounter with Daniel today left me with mixed emotions. There's a heaviness to him now, a shadow that wasn't there before. Walking back through the cobblestone streets with Kanchana and Naureen, I couldn't help but reflect on how much we've all changed. The historic district felt almost ethereal, like a bridge between the past and present. Our shared workspace, with its comforting scent of old books, was a welcome refuge. Daniel hinted at a 'great discovery,' possibly related to the Lost Chronicles. If true, it could be monumental.

We're preparing for a journey to Ur, a place tied to ancient myths. It's exciting but also nerve- wracking. Can we really trust Daniel again?

Kanchana:

Seeing Daniel again today stirred up so many emotions. The café meeting was tense but necessary. We need his help to catch The Mastermind, and he needs our help to clear his name. Walking back with Elodie and Naureen, I couldn't stop thinking about the implications.

Daniel's discovery might be linked to the Lost Chronicles, a project we all were passionate about before everything fell apart. We spent the day planning our next steps, diving back into old research. Naureen found a lead pointing to Ur, an ancient city. It feels like we're on the brink of something huge. Tomorrow, we set off on a new adventure, hoping to uncover the truth and maybe, just maybe, find redemption along the way.

Chapter 17: Secrets Beneath the Sands

The journey to Ur was both exhilarating and exhausting. Kanchana, Elodie , and Naureen had spent days traveling, their excitement growing with each mile that brought them closer to the ancient city. The plane ride was followed by a long drive through the desert, the vast expanse of sand and rock stretching endlessly in every direction.

Finally, they arrived at their destination, an archaeological site on the outskirts of modern-day Nasiriyah. The site was a hive of activity, with researchers and workers bustling about, their movements framed by the backdrop of ancient ziggurats and crumbling ruins.

Dr. Rashid Al-Saadi, the head archaeologist, greeted them warmly. He was a tall, wiry man with sharp features and a kind smile, his eyes twinkling with the passion of a lifelong scholar.

"Welcome to Ur," he said, shaking their hands. "I've heard a lot about your work. It's an honour to have you here."

Kanchana smiled, her eyes scanning the site with eager curiosity. "Thank you, Dr. Al-Saadi. We're excited to be here. We've come across some information that might be related to your recent discoveries."

Dr. Al-Saadi's eyebrows shot up in interest. "Is that so? Come, let's talk in my tent."

They followed him to a large, canvas tent at the edge of the site, its interior filled with tables covered in maps, artifacts, and excavation tools. Dr. Al-Saadi gestured for them to sit, his expression a mix of curiosity and anticipation.

"So, tell me," he said, leaning forward. "What have you discovered?"

Kanchana took a deep breath, her mind racing as she recounted their findings. "We've been researching a collection of ancient texts known as the Lost Chronicles. One of the fragments mentioned a hidden location described as 'where the sun meets the earth.' After cross- referencing various historical and geographical records, we believe this could refer to Ur."

Dr. Al-Saadi's eyes widened. "Fascinating. We've recently uncovered a series of underground chambers here. They appear to be part of a much larger complex, but we haven't been able to access the deeper levels yet."

Elodie leaned forward; her eyes bright with excitement. "Do you think these chambers could be connected to the Lost Chronicles?"

Dr. Al-Saadi nodded slowly. "It's possible. The inscriptions we've found suggest they were used to store something of great importance. If your theory is correct, the Lost Chronicles could be hidden within."

Naureen's heart raced. "What do we need to do to access the deeper chambers?"

Dr. Al-Saadi smiled, a glint of determination in his eyes. "We'll need to dig, carefully and methodically. And we'll need all the help we can get."

The next few days were a blur of activity. Kanchana, Elodie , and Naureen joined Dr. Al-Saadi and his team in the excavation, working tirelessly under the scorching desert sun. They dug through layers of sand and stone, their progress slow but steady.

Kanchana's hands were blistered and sore, but she didn't mind. The thrill of discovery kept her going. One afternoon, as they were carefully clearing away debris from what appeared to be a sealed entrance, she noticed something unusual.

"Look at this," she said, pointing to a series of intricate carvings on the stone door. "These symbols... they match the ones we found in the Lost Chronicles fragment."

Elodie 's eyes widened. "You're right. This must be it."

Dr. Al-Saadi examined the carvings closely. "It looks like a puzzle. If we can decipher it, we might be able to open the door."

Naureen, ever the problem-solver, studied the symbols intently. "Give me a moment," he said, his mind racing. He traced the symbols with his fingers, muttering to himself as he worked through the possible combinations.

After what felt like an eternity, there was a soft click. The stone door shifted slightly, sending a plume of dust into the air. Naureen grinned triumphantly. "Got it."

They all held their breath as they pushed the door open, revealing a dark, narrow passageway that led deep into the earth. Kanchana felt a shiver of anticipation run down her spine.

"This is it," she whispered. "We're about to uncover something incredible."

The passageway was long and winding, its walls lined with ancient carvings and faded murals. They moved cautiously, their footsteps echoing softly in the confined space. Kanchana held a torch aloft, its flickering light casting eerie shadows on the walls.

Finally, they reached a large, circular chamber. The air was cool and still, and the walls were covered in elaborate frescoes depicting scenes of ancient rituals and celestial events. In the centre of the room stood a stone pedestal, upon which rested a large, ornate chest.

Kanchana's heart pounded in her chest as she approached the chest. She could feel the weight of history pressing down on her, the significance of this moment almost overwhelming.

With trembling hands, she lifted the lid. Inside, nestled among layers of delicate silk, were a series of ancient scrolls, their surfaces covered in intricate script.

"The Lost Chronicles," Elodie breathed, her eyes wide with awe. "We found them."

Naureen gently lifted one of the scrolls, his hands steady despite the gravity of the discovery. "This is going to change everything."

Dr. Al-Saadi smiled, his eyes shining with pride and excitement. "You've done it. This is a monumental discovery."

Kanchana felt a surge of emotion, tears welling up in her eyes. "We couldn't have done it without you, Dr. Al-Saadi. Thank you."

He shook his head. "No, thank you. This is a victory for all of us. For history."

They stood together in the ancient chamber, their hearts united by a shared passion and a common goal. In that moment, they were not just historians or archaeologists. They were explorers, uncovering the secrets of the past and bringing them to light for the world to see. That evening, they gathered around a campfire, the desert night cool and clear above them. The stars shone brightly, a reminder of the vastness of the universe and the endless possibilities it held.

Kanchana, Elodie , Naureen, and Dr. Al-Saadi sat together, the warmth of the fire and the camaraderie of their shared adventure filling them with a sense of contentment.

"We've accomplished something incredible," Kanchana said, her voice soft but filled with pride. "But this is just the beginning. There's so much more to discover."

Elodie nodded, her eyes reflecting the firelight. "And we'll do it together. As a team."

Naureen raised his glass, a smile spreading across his face. "To the Lost Chronicles. And to the future."

They clinked their glasses together, the sound ringing out into the night. The journey ahead was uncertain, but they knew they could face it, united by their passion for history and their unwavering bond.

As the fire crackled and the stars shone above, they felt a sense of peace and purpose. The past had revealed its secrets, and the future beckoned with new adventures and discoveries. Together, they would continue their quest, driven by the promise of the unknown and the thrill of the chase.

Trio's diary:

Dear Diary,

Elodie :

The journey to Ur was beyond anything I had imagined. From the plane ride to the long drive through the desert, each moment was filled with exhaustion and exhilaration. I felt like I was stepping into a different world when we arrived at the archaeological site. Dr. Rashid Al- Saadi welcomed us warmly, and I immediately felt the energy and excitement of the bustling site. Kanchana's theory about Ur being linked to the Lost Chronicles seemed more plausible with every passing minute. Today, as we uncovered intricate carvings and finally opened a hidden passage, I couldn't help but think about the enormity of our discovery. The Lost Chronicles were there, right in front of us, waiting to be unveiled. It's hard to believe we're part of something so monumental.

Naureen:

Today was a day I'll never forget. Our journey to Ur was long and tiring, but the moment we arrived at the archaeological site, I knew it was all worth it. Dr. Al-Saadi was incredibly welcoming, and we quickly got to work. Kanchana's theory about the Lost Chronicles possibly being hidden here was spot on. The site itself was amazing, with ancient ruins and ziggurats creating a backdrop of history come alive. After hours of careful excavation under the hot sun, we discovered a sealed entrance with intricate carvings. Solving the puzzle on the door and uncovering the passage felt like a scene from a movie. Finding the Lost Chronicles inside a hidden chamber was the culmination of all our hard work and dedication. It's moments like these that make everything worthwhile.

Kanchana:

Arriving at Ur felt like stepping into a dream. The journey was long and exhausting, but the excitement only grew as we got closer to the ancient city. Dr. Al-Saadi greeted us with such warmth, and his enthusiasm was contagious. Seeing the archaeological site and knowing that we were on the brink of a significant discovery was thrilling. The day was filled with hard work and careful excavation, but every blister and sore muscle was worth it. When we uncovered the intricate carvings and managed to open the sealed door, revealing the passageway, my heart raced with anticipation. Entering the chamber and finding the Lost Chronicles was a moment of pure triumph. This discovery is not just a professional milestone but a testament to our perseverance and passion for history. Tonight, as we sit around the campfire under the stars, I feel an overwhelming sense of pride and contentment. We've achieved something incredible, and the journey ahead promises even more adventures.

Chapter 18: The Enigma of Blackwood Manor

The air was thick with the scent of rain-soaked earth as Kanchana Desai, Elodie Laurent, and Naureen Mehra stood at the entrance of Blackwood Manor. The old mansion, nestled deep within the foggy woods, was a picture of Gothic splendour, with ivy crawling up its stone walls and turrets piercing the grey sky. They had been called here by a mysterious letter, promising the discovery of an ancient artifact linked to the manor's dark history.

"Who do you think sent the letter?" Elodie asked, her voice barely a whisper as she gazed at the imposing structure.

Kanchana shook her head. "I have no idea, but whoever it was knew exactly how to pique our interest. Let's find out what this is all about."

They pushed open the creaky iron gate and made their way up the overgrown path to the manor's grand entrance. The heavy wooden door groaned in protest as Naureen shoved it open, revealing a dimly lit foyer lined with portraits of stern-looking ancestors.

Inside, the air was musty, filled with the scent of old wood and the faint, lingering aroma of lavender. Kanchana, always the most perceptive, noticed a small envelope lying on a dusty table in the centre of the room. She picked it up and read aloud:

"Welcome to Blackwood Manor. Your journey begins in the library. There, you will find the first clue. Proceed with caution."

Naureen raised an eyebrow. "This is starting to feel like a treasure hunt." Elodie smiled. "Exactly our kind of adventure."

The trio followed the dimly lit hallway to the library, a vast room filled with towering bookshelves and ancient tomes. In the centre of the room, on a mahogany desk, lay an old, leather-bound book with a peculiar symbol embossed on the cover.

Kanchana carefully opened the book, revealing a map of the manor grounds with several locations marked. A note was tucked inside, written in elegant, flowing script:

"To uncover the truth, you must solve the riddles. The first clue lies beneath the guardian's watchful gaze."

Elodie frowned. "Guardian's watchful gaze? Any ideas?"

Naureen scanned the room, his eyes landing on a large portrait of a stern man in a military uniform. "That looks like a guardian to me."

They approached the portrait and, after a thorough inspection, discovered a small, hidden compartment behind it. Inside was an ornate key and another note:

"Proceed to the cellar, where shadows dwell and secrets linger."

Armed with the key, they made their way to the cellar. The descent was eerie, with the sound of dripping water echoing through the stone staircase. The cellar was vast, filled with old wine barrels and cobweb-covered crates. In the far corner, they found an old chest, locked, and covered in dust.

Kanchana inserted the key and, with a click, the chest opened to reveal a collection of old manuscripts and a peculiar, glowing artifact. It was a small, intricately carved stone, pulsing with a soft blue light.

Elodie 's eyes widened. "Is this what we were meant to find?"

Kanchana nodded, carefully lifting the stone. "It must be. But what is it?"

As they examined the stone, a voice echoed through the cellar, startling them. "You have done well to find the Heart of Blackwood."

They turned to see an elderly woman standing at the entrance to the cellar, her eyes glinting with a mixture of wisdom and sorrow.

"I am Eliza Blackwood, the last of my line," she said. "The Heart of Blackwood is a powerful artifact, capable of revealing the past and protecting the future. It has been passed down through generations, hidden from those who would misuse its power."

Kanchana stepped forward. "Why did you call us here?"

Eliza smiled sadly. "Because I am old, and my time is near. I needed to find someone worthy to protect the Heart and uncover its secrets. Your reputation as dedicated historians and seekers of truth made you the perfect choice."

Elodie looked at the glowing stone, awe in her eyes. "What should we do with it?"

"Use it wisely," Eliza said. "The Heart can reveal the hidden truths of history, but it can also be dangerous if it falls into the wrong hands. Keep it safe, and let it guide you to uncover the mysteries of the past."

With that, Eliza turned and walked away, leaving the trio in stunned silence. They returned to their headquarters, the Heart of Blackwood safely in Kanchana's bag, their minds racing with the possibilities of what they had discovered.

In the weeks that followed, they delved into the Heart's secrets, uncovering forgotten histories and lost knowledge. The artifact led them on new adventures, each discovery deepening their understanding of the past and its impact on the present.

As they sat in their study, the Heart of Blackwood glowing softly on the table between them, they knew their lives had changed forever. The shadows of the past had unveiled their secrets, and with the Heart's guidance, Kanchana, Elodie , and Naureen were more determined than ever to continue their quest for truth, no Naureener where it led them.

Trio's diary:

Dear Diary, Naureen:

We arrived at Blackwood Manor today, called by a mysterious letter promising the discovery of an ancient artifact. The manor itself is a grand, Gothic structure, full of history and secrets. As soon as we entered, we were led on a treasure hunt through the house, deciphering clues that took us from the library to the cellar. It felt like a movie. Kanchana found the first clue beneath a portrait, and together we unlocked an ancient chest in the cellar. Inside, we discovered the Heart of Blackwood, a glowing artifact said to reveal hidden truths. Meeting Eliza Blackwood, the last of her line, added a layer of solemnity to the adventure. She entrusted us with the Heart, and now we're back at headquarters, diving into its secrets. This could change everything we know about history.

Kanchana:

Today was surreal. Blackwood Manor is everything I'd imagined – dark, mysterious, and brimming with history. The letter that led us here was intriguing enough, but the treasure hunt that ensued was beyond exciting. We deciphered clues and finally found the Heart of Blackwood, a powerful artifact hidden in the cellar. Meeting Eliza Blackwood was like stepping into a different era. She entrusted us with the Heart, saying it could reveal the past and protect the future. I feel a huge sense of responsibility and a tinge of excitement about what we might uncover next. This is what we live for – the thrill of discovery and the promise of new adventures.

Elodie :

Blackwood Manor was like something out of a gothic novel. The letter that brought us here set us on an intriguing path, solving riddles that led us to the Heart of Blackwood. The library was a historian's dream, and the cellar where we found the artifact felt like uncovering buried treasure. Meeting Eliza Blackwood and learning about the artifact's significance was incredible. She believes in our ability to protect and use it wisely. Back at our headquarters, the Heart of Blackwood sits on our table, glowing softly, full of secrets waiting to be unveiled. I can't help but feel a mix of awe and anticipation. This discovery is monumental, and I can't wait to see where it leads us.

Chapter 19: The Enigma of the Stone Circle

The early morning fog still clung to the hills as Kanchana Desai, Elodie Laurent, and Naureen Mehra made their way to the ancient stone circle known as Ravenshire Ring. Shrouded in mystery and legend, the site was rumoured to be a place of great historical significance.

Recently, a farmer had discovered what appeared to be an ancient artifact buried near the stones, and the trio had been called in to investigate.

As they approached the site, the towering stones loomed over them, their weathered surfaces etched with indecipherable runes. Kanchana, ever the keen observer, felt a shiver of excitement. "There's something special about this place," she said, her voice tinged with awe.

Elodie nodded, her eyes scanning the landscape. "These stones have witnessed countless events. If only they could talk."

Naureen, carrying their equipment, grinned. "That's our job—to make the past speak."

They set up their makeshift base near the centre of the circle, unloading tools and notebooks. The artifact, a small, intricately carved stone tablet, lay on a cloth in the middle. Kanchana picked it up, running her fingers over the symbols.

"This is definitely ancient," she said, "but I can't recognize the script. It's not like anything I've seen before."

Elodie leaned in, her brow furrowing. "It looks almost like a mix of Celtic and Norse runes. Could this be some form of hybrid language?"

Naureen took a photo of the tablet. "We'll need to cross-reference these symbols with our database. But first, let's see if we can find any clues around the stones."

The trio split up, each examining different parts of the circle. Kanchana focused on the central stone, a massive monolith that seemed to pulse with a faint energy. As she circled it, she noticed a series of tiny holes drilled into the base, forming a pattern.

"Elodie , Naureen, come here!" she called out. "I think I've found something."

They rushed over, and Elodie immediately recognized the pattern. "It's a star map. These holes represent constellations."

Naureen's eyes lit up. "So, this circle might have been used for astronomical observations. But why?"

Kanchana pondered for a moment. "Ancient cultures often used the stars to navigate and mark important events. Maybe this circle was a kind of calendar or a place for rituals connected to celestial events."

Elodie added, "And the tablet could be a key to understanding how it all worked."

They spent the next few hours meticulously documenting the positions of the holes and comparing them to star charts. As the sun climbed higher, Naureen's phone buzzed with a message from their colleague, Dr. Emily Hartwell, back at the university.

"I sent her the symbols," Naureen explained. "Let's see what she found."

He read aloud: "The symbols are a mix of Old Norse and an unknown script, possibly pre- Celtic. One of the phrases translates to 'The Gate of Worlds.'"

Kanchana's eyes widened. "The Gate of Worlds? That sounds like something out of a legend."

Elodie nodded. "There are stories about places where the veil between our world and other realms is thin. What if Ravenshire Ring is one of those places?"

Naureen looked around, a newfound respect for the ancient stones evident on his face. "If that's true, this place could be even more significant than we thought. But how do we prove it?"

Kanchana had an idea. "Let's wait until nightfall and see if anything happens when the stars align with the pattern on the stone."

As dusk fell, the trio prepared for their night vigil. The temperature dropped, and the air grew still, the only sounds the rustling of leaves and the occasional hoot of an owl. They sat in a circle around the central stone, their eyes fixed on the sky.

Hours passed, and the stars slowly moved into alignment with the holes in the stone. Suddenly, the ground beneath them began to hum, a low vibration that grew stronger as the stars perfectly aligned.

Elodie gasped. "Look at the central stone!"

The monolith was glowing, faint lines of light tracing the pattern of the star map. The tablet in Kanchana's hands warmed, and the symbols began to glow as well.

"This is incredible," Naureen whispered. "It's like the stones are activating."

As the glow intensified, a soft, ethereal light filled the circle. The air felt charged with energy, and the trio watched in awe as a faint image appeared above the central stone—an ancient map, showing lands and places long forgotten.

Kanchana, Elodie , and Naureen exchanged stunned looks. Kanchana spoke first, her voice filled with wonder. "We've unlocked something extraordinary. This isn't just a stone circle—it's a gateway to understanding our ancient past."

Elodie nodded, her eyes shining with excitement. "And maybe even to other worlds." Naureen grinned, his earlier scepticism replaced by awe. "This is going to rewrite history."

As the glow slowly faded, the trio knew that their discovery at Ravenshire Ring was just the beginning. The Gate of Worlds had opened a new chapter in their quest for knowledge, promising more adventures and revelations to come.

With renewed determination, they packed up their equipment, ready to delve deeper into the mysteries of the ancient world. The journey was far from over, and together, they would uncover the secrets that lay hidden in the shadows of the past.

Trio's diary:

Dear Diary, Naureen:

Today was incredible. We arrived at Ravenshire Ring; an ancient stone circle shrouded in mystery. The site was as awe-inspiring as the legends said, with towering stones covered in ancient runes. We were there to investigate an artifact found by a local farmer—a small, intricately carved stone tablet. The script on it was unlike anything we'd seen, a mix of Celtic and Norse runes. As we explored, Kanchana discovered a star map etched into one of the stones, indicating the circle might have been used for astronomical observations. At night, as the stars aligned with the holes in the stone, the ground began to hum, and the central stone glowed, revealing an ancient map of forgotten lands. This discovery is monumental—it feels like we've unlocked a gateway to understanding our ancient past. I can't wait to see where this leads us next.

Kanchana:

Ravenshire Ring took my breath away today. The ancient stone circle, veiled in mist, held an undeniable aura of mystery and history. The artifact we came to investigate—a stone tablet with an unknown script—turned out to be even more fascinating than we thought. As we explored, we found a star map on the central stone, suggesting the site was used for celestial observations. Tonight, as the stars aligned, the stone glowed, and the tablet in my hands warmed and glowed as well. The stones seemed to activate, revealing an ethereal image of an ancient map. This place is a gateway to the past, and perhaps to other worlds. The Gate of Worlds—it's like stepping into a legend. This discovery will change everything. I feel more determined than ever to uncover the secrets of our ancient history.

Elodie :

Today at Ravenshire Ring was nothing short of magical. The ancient stone circle, with its towering monoliths and mysterious runes, was captivating. We were there to investigate a stone tablet found by a farmer, its script was a blend of Celtic and Norse runes. As we explored, Kanchana discovered a star map on the central stone, hinting at its use for astronomical purposes. As night fell and the stars aligned, the ground hummed, and the central stone glowed, revealing an ancient map above it. The tablet in Kanchana's hands glowed too. It felt like the stones were alive, activating under the starlight. This place is extraordinary—it's the Gate of Worlds, a link to ancient knowledge and possibly other realms. This discovery is going to rewrite history, and I'm thrilled to be part of it. The journey is just beginning, and I can't wait to uncover more.

.

Chapter 20: The Guardians of Ravenshire

The news of their discovery at Ravenshire Ring had spread quickly, drawing attention from scholars, media, and even local legend keepers. Kanchana, Elodie , and Naureen were at the centre of a growing storm of interest and speculation. Yet, they remained focused on deciphering the ancient map and unlocking the full potential of the Gate of Worlds.

One evening, as they were poring over the map's details in their Victorian headquarters, a knock on the door interrupted their concentration. Kanchana opened it to reveal an elderly woman, her face lined with age but her eyes sharp and penetrating.

"Good evening," the woman said, her voice strong despite her years. "I am Agnes Wren, keeper of the local lore. I hear you have awakened the Gate."

Elodie and Naureen exchanged surprised glances, but Kanchana stepped aside to let Agnes in. "Please, come in. We have many questions."

Agnes settled into a chair by the fire, her presence commanding their attention. "The Ravenshire Ring has long been a place of power," she began. "Few know its true purpose, but my ancestors were its guardians. The map you saw is only the beginning. The Gate can connect our world to others, but it also safeguards great dangers."

Kanchana leaned forward, her curiosity piqued. "What kind of dangers?"

Agnes looked at her, eyes gleaming with ancient knowledge. "There are realms beyond our understanding, filled with both wonders and perils. The Gate was built to control the flow between these worlds. Without proper knowledge, opening it fully could bring disaster."

Naureen frowned. "Then why leave the map and clues for us to find?"

"The map is a test," Agnes explained. "Only those with pure intent and wisdom can decipher it. You have shown that you are worthy, but you must be cautious."

Elodie nodded, absorbing the gravity of Agnes's words. "So, what do we do next?"

Agnes smiled faintly. "You must seek the other guardians. They hold pieces of knowledge and artifacts necessary to control the Gate safely. The first guardian lives in the remote highlands of Scotland. His name is Eamon MacLeod."

The trio exchanged determined looks. They knew their journey was far from over and that finding Eamon was their next step.

A week later, Kanchana, Elodie , and Naureen found themselves trekking through the rugged landscapes of the Scottish highlands. The air was crisp and the scenery breathtaking, but their minds were focused on the task at hand.

After a gruelling hike, they arrived at a secluded cottage nestled between two hills. An elderly man, tall and robust despite his age, greeted them at the door.

"Eamon MacLeod?" Kanchana asked.

The man nodded. "Aye, that's me. You must be the ones Agnes spoke of."

They were invited inside, where the warmth of a roaring fire and the smell of freshly baked bread greeted them. Eamon wasted no time, handing them a worn leather-bound journal.

"This contains my family's knowledge of the Gate," he explained. "But knowledge alone isn't enough. You must prove your worth by completing a challenge—retrieving the Heartstone from the Cave of Echoes."

Elodie 's eyes widened. "The Heartstone? What's that?"

Eamon's expression grew serious. "The Heartstone is a powerful artifact, essential for stabilizing the Gate. It lies deep within the cave, protected by trials that test your courage, wisdom, and unity."

The next morning, equipped with Eamon's journal and their determination, the trio set off for the Cave of Echoes. The entrance was hidden behind a waterfall, the roar of water masking any sound from within. They pushed through the curtain of water, emerging into a dimly lit cavern.

As they ventured deeper, the cave's natural beauty gave way to a series of daunting challenges. The first trial was a labyrinth of narrow passages. With Naureen's keen sense of direction and Elodie's attention to detail, they navigated the maze, finding clues etched into the walls that guided their way.

The second trial tested their courage. They entered a chamber filled with deep chasms, with only a few unstable stone bridges to cross. Kanchana's steady nerves and Naureen's physical agility got them through, while Elodie 's calm presence kept their spirits high.

Finally, they reached the last chamber, where the Heartstone rested on a pedestal. But as they approached, the ground trembled, and spectral guardians emerged from the shadows.

Kanchana stepped forward, recalling Eamon's advice. "Show respect and speak the ancient words," she instructed.

Together, they recited a passage from Eamon's journal. The guardians paused, their forms flickering, before bowing and retreating into the darkness. The trio approached the pedestal, and Kanchana carefully lifted the Heartstone, its surface warm and pulsating with energy.

Returning to Eamon's cottage, they presented the Heartstone. Eamon nodded in approval, his eyes reflecting a mix of relief and pride.

"You've done well," he said. "With the Heartstone, you can stabilize the Gate. But remember, this is just the beginning. Many more guardians and trials await you."

As they prepared to leave, Eamon handed them a small, intricately carved box. "This will guide you to the next guardian. Trust in each other and in your quest."

With renewed purpose, Kanchana, Elodie , and Naureen set off, ready to face whatever challenges lay ahead. The enigma of the Gate of Worlds was beginning to unfold, and they were determined to uncover its secrets and protect its power.

Their journey continued, the shadows of the past guiding them toward a future filled with both peril and promise. Together, they would navigate the intricate web of history, unlocking the mysteries of the Gate and safeguarding the legacy of Ravenshire Ring.

Trio's diary:

Dear Diary, Kanchana:

The discovery at Ravenshire Ring has set off a chain of events that I could never have imagined. Tonight, we had an unexpected visitor: Agnes Wren, a local lore keeper. She told us about the true purpose of the Ravenshire Ring and the potential dangers it holds. The Gate of Worlds is not just a myth; it's real and powerful. Agnes warned us about the perils of other realms and entrusted us with the task of finding other guardians who hold crucial knowledge and artifacts. Our first stop is Scotland, to meet Eamon MacLeod. The journey ahead is daunting, but with Elodie and Naureen by my side, I feel ready to face whatever comes next.

Elodie :

Today was extraordinary. We were visited by Agnes Wren, a guardian of the Ravenshire Ring's secrets. She revealed that the site is a gateway between worlds and that we must seek out other guardians to safely harness its power. Our first destination is the Scottish Highlands, where we'll meet Eamon MacLeod. The journey is already proving to be more than just about ancient history; it's about protecting the future. I'm excited and a bit anxious, but I trust

Kanchana and Naureen completely. Together, we will navigate these new challenges.

Naureen:

The past few days have been a whirlwind. After our discovery at Ravenshire Ring, Agnes Wren visited us. She explained that the site is a powerful gateway and warned us of the dangers it holds. Our mission is to find other guardians, starting with Eamon MacLeod in Scotland. Today, we trekked through the rugged highlands to find him. Eamon was expecting us, thanks to Agnes. He tasked us with retrieving the Heartstone from the Cave of Echoes. It was a gruelling challenge, testing our courage, wisdom, and unity. We succeeded and brought the

Heartstone back to Eamon. This artifact is vital for stabilizing the Gate. Our journey is just beginning, and I am ready to uncover more secrets and protect this incredible discovery.

Chapter 21: Afternoon Tea with the Siblings

The countryside cottage where the siblings, Dr. Zayd Hasan and Mrs. Laila Reilly lived was nestled in a quaint village, surrounded by lush gardens and ancient trees. The summer air was warm, carrying the sweet scent of blooming flowers. Kanchana, Elodie , and Naureen had been invited to spend the afternoon with the siblings, now retired and settled with their spouses, sharing stories and wisdom accumulated over their long and illustrious careers.

As they approached the charming cottage, Kanchana could not help but smile at the sight of the vibrant garden. It was clear that Laila 's touch was everywhere, from the meticulously maintained flowerbeds to the welcoming pathway lined with blooming roses. The front door swung open before they had a chance to knock, and Laila , still graceful and elegant despite her years, greeted them with a warm smile.

"Welcome, welcome! Come in, we have been eagerly waiting for you," Laila said, her voice filled with genuine warmth.

They followed her into the cozy living room, where Dr. Zayd Hasan, though visibly older and frailer, rose to greet them. His eyes still sparkled with the same intellectual curiosity that had driven his work for decades.

"It's good to see you all," Zayd said, his voice slightly raspy but filled with sincerity. "Please, make yourselves at home."

They exchanged pleasantries, and soon the room was filled with the pleasant aroma of freshly brewed tea and scones. Zayd's wife (Evelyn) and daughters (Samira and Sara), and Laila's husband (Sahil) and children (Omar and Rami), joined them, their presence adding to the familial atmosphere.

The group settled around a large wooden table in the garden, shaded by a canopy of wisteria. As they sipped their tea and nibbled on sandwiches and scones, the conversation flowed easily. Zayd and Laila shared stories of their adventures and discoveries, their eyes lighting up with each tale.

Kanchana listened intently, occasionally glancing at Elodie and Naureen, who were equally engrossed. Despite the peaceful setting, she could not help but notice the way Zayd coughed occasionally, a deep, rattling sound that seemed to take more out of him each time.

"Zayd, are you feeling alright?" Elodie asked gently, her concern evident.

"Yes Dad, are you ok?", Samira, with anticipation, gently asked

Zayd waved a hand dismissively, though it was clear he was struggling. "Just a bit of a cold, nothing to worry about."

Evelyn's worried glance at her husband suggested otherwise, but the conversation continued. As the afternoon wore on, Zayd shared more about their latest findings before retirement, and Laila talked about the importance of preserving historical sites.

Kanchana found herself inspired by their dedication, even in their twilight years. She could see the same passion for discovery in Elodie and Naureen's eyes, a reflection of their own commitment to uncovering the past.

As the sun began to dip towards the horizon, casting a golden hue over the garden, Zayd's coughing grew more frequent and severe. Laila and Evelyn exchanged a worried look, and Sahil suggested they move inside.

Once settled in the living room, Zayd's condition seemed to worsen. Evelyn fetched his medication, but it was clear that he needed to rest. The atmosphere grew sombre as they realized the extent of his illness.

"We've been through a lot together," Zayd said, his voice weaker now. "But I'm afraid my journey is nearing its end."

Kanchana felt a lump in her throat. "You've accomplished so much, Zayd. Your work will continue to inspire us all."

Zayd smiled faintly. "Thank you, Kanchana. That means a lot."

As the evening grew darker, Laila and Sahil showed their guests to their rooms. They had insisted on staying the night, given the late hour and Zayd's condition. The trio sat together in the guest room, the weight of the day's events heavy on their minds.

"Zayd and Laila have given so much to the world," Elodie said softly. "We have to make sure their legacy lives on."

Naureen nodded. "We will. Everything they've taught us, we'll carry it forward."

Kanchana looked at her friends, her resolve strengthening. "And we'll do it together, just as they've always done."

That night, they wrote in their diaries, reflecting on the day's events and the lessons they had learned.

The next morning, the sun rose gently over the cottage, casting a warm, golden light through the windows. Zayd, though still visibly weak, insisted on joining them for breakfast.

"It's important to me," he said, his voice trembling slightly but filled with determination. "One more morning with friends, sharing our love for history and discovery."

They gathered around the breakfast table, the mood a mix of sombre reflection and heartfelt camaraderie. Evelyn served a simple yet delicious meal of fresh fruit, pastries, and eggs.

Zayd shared more stories from his past, each word carefully chosen, as if he were imparting final pieces of wisdom to his friends.

"There's one last thing I need to show you," Zayd said after they had finished eating. He led them to his study, a room filled with books, maps, and artifacts collected over decades. On the desk lay an old, leather-bound journal, its pages yellowed with age.

"This journal contains my life's work," Zayd explained. "Notes, observations, theories— everything I've discovered about the Gate of Worlds. I want you to have it."

Kanchana accepted the journal with reverence, understanding the significance of the gift. "Thank you, Zayd. We will treasure it and continue your work."

With a nod, Zayd sat back in his chair, visibly exhausted but content. "Take good care of each other and always seek the truth. The past holds many secrets, and it's our duty to uncover them."

Later that day, after ensuring Zayd was comfortable, Kanchana, Elodie , and Naureen decided to explore the garden once more. The vibrant blooms and the gentle hum of bees provided a stark contrast to the heavy emotions they carried.

"Even in his final days, Zayd is teaching us," Kanchana said, her voice filled with admiration.

"He's a remarkable man," Elodie agreed. "And Laila too. Their dedication to history and each other is inspiring."

As they wandered through the garden, they discussed their plans. They knew that continuing Zayd and Laila 's work would be a significant undertaking, but they were determined to honour their mentors' legacy.

That evening, they gathered in the living room again, this time joined by Laila and Sahil. The conversation turned to lighter topics, stories of past adventures, and shared laughter.

Despite the underlying sadness, there was a sense of unity and purpose that bound them all together.

As night fell, Kanchana, Elodie , and Naureen retired to their rooms, their hearts heavy but their resolve firm. They spent some time writing in their diaries, capturing the emotions and reflections of the past two days.

Trio's diary:

Dear Diary, Kanchana:

Today was both heartwarming and heartbreaking. Spending time with Zayd and Laila was a reminder of why we do what we do. Their stories, their passion, it's all so inspiring. But seeing Zayd so ill was difficult. I hope we can make them proud by continuing their work. We must keep pushing forward, uncovering the secrets of the past and safeguarding them for the future.

Elodie :

Meeting Zayd and Laila today was a profound experience. They have dedicated their lives to uncovering history and preserving it. It was wonderful to see them so happy and settled, but Zayd's illness is a stark reminder of our mortality. We must ensure that their legacy is honoured and that their contributions to history are never forgotten.

Naureen:

Today was a mix of joy and sorrow. Zayd and Laila 's home is filled with love and history, a testament to their life's work. Zayd's condition worries me, but it also strengthens my resolve to carry on their legacy. We have a responsibility to continue their work, to keep the past alive and learn from it. Together, we can achieve great things.

Chapter 22: A Chance Encounter

The sunbathed the schoolyard in a golden glow as Kanchana, Elodie , and Naureen meandered through the familiar grounds of their old primary school. Laughter and shouts echoed from the playground, a nostalgic reminder of the carefree days of their youth. As they ambled past the rows of classrooms, lost in reminiscence, they turned a corner and stumbled upon an unexpected sight—their former teachers, Mrs. Laila Reilly, and Dr. Zayd Hasan, still hard at work despite the passage of time.

"Mrs. Reilly, Dr. Hasan! What a delightful surprise!" Kanchana exclaimed, genuine warmth in her voice as she greeted the two educators who had left an indelible mark on their lives.

Laila 's eyes sparkled with joy as she embraced each of them in turn. "Oh, it's lovely to see you all again! What brings you back to our humble abode?"

"We were just taking a stroll down memory lane," Elodie replied, her smile bright with nostalgia. "It's been ages since we last visited."

Zayd, leaning lightly on his cane, nodded in agreement. "Ah, the memories we've shared within these walls. It's heartwarming to see the school thriving as it always has."

Their conversation flowed effortlessly as they exchanged updates on their lives and reminisced about the past. However, Kanchana couldn't shake the nagging concern that lingered at the back of her mind. She noticed the slight tremor in Zayd's hands and the weariness etched into Laila 's expression. Something was amiss, and Kanchana was determined to get to the bottom of it.

"Dr. Hasan, you seem a bit fatigued. Are you feeling alright?" Naureen's voice was laced with genuine concern as he addressed their former mentor.

Zayd attempted to wave off their worries with a dismissive chuckle. "Oh, just a touch of old age catching up with me, I'm afraid. Nothing to worry about."

But Kanchana saw through the facade. She remembered the severity of Zayd's coughing fits from their last encounter, and she knew they couldn't afford to ignore the signs of his declining health.

"Perhaps it's time for you to take a break, Zayd," she suggested gently. "You've dedicated so much of your life to teaching and guiding us. Let us take care of you for a change."

Zayd hesitated, but Laila 's reassuring touch on his arm encouraged him to relent. "Perhaps you're right. It may be time for a bit of respite."

They escorted Zayd and Laila back to their cozy home, the worry for Zayd's health weighing heavily on their minds. Kanchana couldn't shake the feeling of unease as they bid their mentors farewell, promising to check in on them regularly.

Later that evening, as they sat in their study reflecting on the day's events, Kanchana, Elodie , and Naureen knew they had to take action to help Zayd. They couldn't stand idly by and watch him suffer in silence.

With a shared determination, Kanchana, Elodie , and Naureen resolved to visit Zayd the following day and extend their help in any way possible. They knew that their esteemed mentor had always been there for them, guiding them with wisdom and patience. Now it was their turn to reciprocate the care and support Zayd had given them, ensuring that he received the assistance and comfort he deserved in his time of need.

Trio's Diary

Dear Diary, Kanchana:

Today was both heartwarming and concerning. Seeing Mrs. Reilly and Dr. Hasan again brings back floods of memories, but it's clear that Zayd isn't doing well. His health is deteriorating, and it's troubling to witness someone we admire and respect struggling. We must find a way to support him, to repay all that he's done for us over the years.

Elodie :

Meeting Mrs. Reilly and Dr. Hasan today was a bittersweet experience. They were such an integral part of our lives, and it's disheartening to witness them aging. Zayd's declining health is a cause for concern, and I can't shake the feeling that we need to do something to assist him. We owe him so much for all he's taught us.

Naureen:

Today's encounter with Mrs. Reilly and Dr. Hasan was entirely unexpected. It's evident that Zayd isn't doing well, and it pains me to see him struggling. We must find a way to offer him our support, to demonstrate how much he means to us. He's been a mentor and a friend, and we owe him our gratitude and assistance in his time of need.

Chapter 23: Shadows of Concern

The invitation from Eliza Blackwood to Blackwood Manor had sparked a mixture of excitement and curiosity in Kanchana, Elodie , and Naureen. As they made their way to the ancient estate, nestled amidst the sprawling woodlands, they couldn't shake the feeling of anticipation tinged with apprehension.

Upon their arrival, they were greeted by the solemn grandeur of the manor, its imposing facade shrouded in the fading light of dusk. Eliza, the keeper of the manor's secrets, welcomed them with a sombre expression, her eyes betraying a hint of urgency.

"Thank you for coming, my dear friends," Eliza said, her voice tinged with concern. "There is much we need to discuss."

They followed Eliza into the grand parlour, where a fire crackled in the hearth, casting flickering shadows on the ornate furnishings. Kanchana, Elodie , and Naureen exchanged curious glances, sensing the gravity of the situation.

"Please, take a seat," Eliza said, gesturing towards the plush armchairs arranged around the room. "I'm afraid there's no easy way to broach this topic, but it concerns the safety of the Gate of Worlds."

Kanchana's heart skipped a beat. "What's happened?"

Eliza sighed, her gaze troubled. "There have been disturbances—ominous signs that the balance of the Gate is being threatened. I fear that darker forces are at play, seeking to exploit its power for their own ends."

Elodie 's brow furrowed in concern. "But how can we protect it? What can we do?"

Eliza fixed them with a steady gaze. "You are the guardians of the Gate, entrusted with its safety and preservation. But you cannot face this threat alone. You will need allies— others who understand the significance of the Gate and are willing to defend it at all costs."

Before they could respond, Kanchana's phone rang, breaking the tense silence. It was Evelyn, Zayd Hasan's wife, her voice trembling with emotion.

"Kanchana, it's Zayd. He's been admitted to the hospital. It's... it's late stage laryngeal and lung cancer."

The news hit them like a sledgehammer, leaving them reeling with shock and disbelief. Zayd, their beloved mentor, and friend, battling a life-threatening illness—it was almost too much to bear.

Kanchana's hands trembled as she struggled to find the right words. "Evelyn, we'll be there right away. Just hold on."

With a heavy heart, Kanchana relayed the devastating news to Elodie and Naureen. Without hesitation, they rushed to the hospital, their minds consumed with worry for Zayd and support for Evelyn.

As they arrived at the hospital, Evelyn, Sara and Samira greeted them with tear-streaked cheeks, their anguish palpable. Kanchana, Elodie , and Naureen enveloped her in a comforting embrace, their solidarity a beacon of hope in the face of despair.

With utter emotion, Sara uttered, "Dad, you can't leave us! Mum, Aunt Jo, there should be something we could do."

The doctor, with an unnoticeable grin, claimed "I'm afraid we can't save him. He only as 10 days."

Zayd lay in the hospital bed, his once vibrant spirit subdued by the weight of his illness. Kanchana, Elodie , and Naureen sat by his side, offering words of encouragement and silent prayers for his recovery.

In that moment, amidst the shadows of uncertainty and fear, they drew strength from their bond—a bond forged through shared experiences, triumphs, and challenges. Together, they would face whatever lay ahead, united in their determination to protect the ones they loved and the legacy they had sworn to defend.

Trio's Diary:

Dear Diary, Kanchana:

Today has been one of the most difficult days of my life. Hearing about Zayd's illness punched my gut—it was a stark reminder of the fragility of life and the uncertainty of tomorrow. But amidst the pain and sorrow, there is a glimmer of hope—the unwavering support of friends and the strength we find in each other's company.

Elodie :

The news of Zayd's illness has left me reeling, my heart heavy with sorrow. He has always been a pillar of strength and wisdom, guiding us through the darkest of times. Now, it's our turn to be there for him, to offer whatever comfort and support we can in his time of need.

Naureen:

Today has been a stark reminder of the fragility of life. The news of Zayd's cancer hit me hard, but it's shown me the importance of cherishing every moment we have with the ones we love.

Together, we'll face whatever challenges lie ahead, drawing strength from our bonds of friendship and the shared determination to overcome adversity. We can pitch into this together.

Chapter 24: Forging a Legacy

Basingstoke, a bustling town steeped in history and tradition, was the setting for Kanchana, Elodie , and Naureen's latest endeavour—a quest that would not only uncover hidden truths but also carve a path into the Elodie ls of history itself. With the weight of Dr. Zayd Hasan's legacy heavy on their shoulders, they were determined to honour his memory in the most profound way possible.

Their journey began with a chance discovery—a forgotten manuscript tucked away in the archives of the local museum. As they pored over its pages, they realized they had stumbled upon a treasure trove of untold stories, forgotten heroes, and lost civilizations.

Eager to share their findings with the world, they embarked on a meticulous research expedition, delving into the depths of history to unearth the secrets buried beneath layers of time and neglect. With each revelation, they felt a sense of awe and wonder, knowing they were on the brink of something extraordinary.

Their efforts did not go unnoticed. News of their groundbreaking discoveries spread like wildfire, capturing the attention of historians, scholars, and enthusiasts alike. Suddenly, Kanchana, Elodie , and Naureen found themselves thrust into the spotlight, their names synonymous with groundbreaking research and groundbreaking achievements.

But their journey was far from over. Fuelled by their passion for uncovering the truth, they pushed forward, determined to leave no stone unturned in their quest for knowledge and understanding. With each new revelation, they forged ahead, undeterred by the obstacles that lay in their path.

Their dedication paid off in ways they could never have imagined. One fateful day, they received a letter—a letter that would change their lives forever. It was an invitation to a prestigious awards ceremony, where they would be honoured for their contributions to the field of historical research.

As they stood on the stage, bathed in the glow of the spotlight, Kanchana, Elodie , and Naureen felt a sense of pride unlike any they had ever known. Here, in front of their peers and colleagues, they were being recognized for their efforts to preserve the past and shape the future.

But the greatest reward was yet to come. As they accepted their awards, they were presented with a check—a check for a sum of money so large it took their breath away. It was a gesture of gratitude, a token of appreciation for their tireless dedication and unwavering commitment to their craft.

As they left the stage, clutching their awards and their prize money, Kanchana, Elodie , and Naureen felt a sense of accomplishment that surpassed anything they had ever experienced. They had not only found history—they had made history, leaving an indelible mark on the world that would be remembered for generations to come.

But amidst the accolades and the applause, their thoughts turned to Dr. Zayd Hasan, the man who had inspired them to embark on this incredible journey. Though he was no longer with them, his spirit lived on in their hearts, guiding them forward and inspiring them to reach new heights of greatness.

As they toasted to their success, raising their glasses in a silent tribute to their mentor and friend, they knew that Dr. Hasan would be proud. Proud of the legacy they had built, proud of the history they had uncovered, and proud of the bright future that lay ahead.

Trio's Diary:

Dear Diary,

Kanchana:

Today has been a whirlwind of emotions, from the exhilaration of our historic achievement to the sobering news of Dr. Hasan's illness. It's a stark reminder that life is a delicate balance of triumphs and tribulations. Our victory feels bittersweet knowing that our dear friend is facing such a difficult battle.

Elodie :

The events of today have left me feeling both elated and heartbroken. To receive such recognition for our work is a dream come true, but it's overshadowed by the news of Dr. Hasan's illness. We must channel this success into something meaningful, not just for ourselves but for him too.

Naureen:

Today has been a rollercoaster of highs and lows. Winning the cash prize is beyond anything we could have imagined, but it's tempered by the news of Dr. Hasan's cancer diagnosis. It's a stark reminder that life can change in an instant, and we must make every moment count. We'll use this prize not just for ourselves but to honour Dr. Hasan's legacy.

Chapter 25: The Path of Discovery

Kanchana, Elodie , and Naureen found themselves gathered once again in their cozy study in Basingstoke, surrounded by stacks of books and maps, their minds buzzing with excitement and anticipation. They had just received an invitation that promised to be the culmination of their years of dedication and hard work—the unveiling of a groundbreaking archaeological discovery that would redefine our understanding of ancient civilizations.

As they sat together, sipping tea and poring over the details of the invitation, a sense of awe and reverence washed over them. This wasn't just another excavation or research project; it was a chance to make history—to be a part of something truly extraordinary.

"The opportunity to witness history being made firsthand is exhilarating," Kanchana remarked, her eyes shining with excitement. "We've dedicated our lives to uncovering the mysteries of the past, and now, we have the chance to witness a discovery that could reshape our understanding of ancient civilizations."

Elodie nodded eagerly, her mind already racing with possibilities. "It's moments like these that remind us why we do what we do. The thrill of discovery, the excitement of uncovering secrets long buried beneath the sands of time—it's what drives us forward, propelling us into the unknown."

Naureen grinned, his enthusiasm palpable. "And what better way to celebrate our passion for history than by being a part of something truly groundbreaking? This isn't just about the artifacts or the accolades—it's about the pursuit of knowledge, the quest for truth, and the unwavering belief that every discovery, no Naureener how small, has the power to change the world."

With their minds made up and their hearts full of anticipation, the trio set about preparing for their journey. They meticulously packed their bags, ensuring they had everything they would need for the expedition ahead—notebooks, cameras, excavation tools, and, most importantly, their insatiable thirst for knowledge.

As they delved into their work, their minds occasionally wandered back to their dear friend, Dr. Zayd Hasan. Thoughts of his illness weighed heavy on their hearts, a constant reminder of the fragility of life and the unpredictability of fate.

Kanchana couldn't shake the image of Zayd, his once vibrant spirit now overshadowed by the spectre of cancer. She found herself consumed by worry, her thoughts drifting back to the countless hours they had spent together, poring over ancient texts, and unravelling the mysteries of the past. Zayd had always been a source of inspiration and guidance, a pillar of strength in times of uncertainty. Now, as he faced his own battle, Kanchana felt a profound sense of helplessness, a longing to ease his suffering and offer whatever comfort she could.

Elodie , too, found herself grappling with a whirlwind of emotions. Zayd had been more than just a colleague—he had been a mentor, a confidant, and a dear friend. The news of his illness had hit her hard, stirring up memories of their shared adventures and the countless conversations they had shared over cups of tea. She couldn't bear the thought of losing him, couldn't imagine a world without his wisdom and guidance. And yet, as she watched him struggle with his illness, Elodie couldn't help but feel a sense of admiration for his resilience and strength. Despite the pain and uncertainty, Zayd remained steadfast in his determination to fight, his spirit unbroken by the trials that lay ahead.

Naureen, too, was deeply affected by Zayd's illness. He had always admired Zayd for his intellect, his passion for discovery, and his unwavering dedication to the pursuit of knowledge. Now, as he watched his friend grapple with the harsh realities of cancer, Naureen felt a profound sense of sadness and frustration. He longed to offer words of comfort and support, to be there for Zayd in his time of need. And yet, as they worked tirelessly to uncover the secrets of the past,

Naureen couldn't help but wonder about the fragility of life and the fleeting nature of existence.

Zayd's illness served as a stark reminder of their own mortality, a sobering realization that no amount of knowledge or expertise could shield them from the uncertainties of the future.

As they continued their work, their thoughts often drifted back to Zayd, a constant presence in their minds and hearts. They found solace in each other's company, drawing strength from their shared determination to make the most of every moment they had together. The trio delved deeper into the mysteries of the past, they vowed to honour Zayd's legacy by embracing life's challenges with courage, resilience, and unwavering determination. In the end, it wasn't just about the discoveries they made or the accolades they received—it was about the bonds they forged, the memories they cherished, and the profound impact they had on each other's lives.

They travelled to the excavation site, surrounded by the beauty and majesty of the natural world, a sense of reverence settled over them. They were about to embark on a journey that would take them to the very heart of ancient history—a journey that would test their resolve, challenge their beliefs, and ultimately redefine their understanding of the world around them.

"I can't help but feel a sense of awe and wonder," Elodie remarked, her eyes scanning the landscape with admiration. "To think that we're about to witness a discovery that could change the course of history—it's truly humbling."

Naureen nodded in agreement, his gaze fixed on the horizon. "And yet, despite the magnitude of what lies ahead, I can't help but feel a sense of excitement. This is what we live for—the thrill of the unknown, the promise of discovery, and the opportunity to leave our mark on the pages of history."

Kanchana smiled, her heart swelling with pride. "And as we stand on the precipice of discovery, ready to embark on this incredible journey, I couldn't imagine doing it with anyone else by my side. Together, we're unstoppable—we're a force to be reckoned with, united in purpose and driven by our shared passion for uncovering the secrets of the past."

As they arrived at the excavation site, the anticipation reached a fever pitch. A team of fellow archaeologists and researchers greeted them, all eager to begin the work ahead. The air was alive with excitement, the atmosphere charged with the promise of discovery.

"Here we are, on the brink of something truly extraordinary," Kanchana remarked, her voice filled with awe. "This is where history is made, where the past comes alive, and where the future begins."

Elodie nodded, her eyes sparkling with anticipation. "And as we prepare to delve into the depths of the unknown, let us never forget the privilege and responsibility that comes with our work. We are the stewards of history, the guardians of knowledge, and the torchbearers of truth."

Naureen grinned, his spirit soaring with excitement. "So let us embrace the challenges that lie ahead, let us face them head-on with courage and determination, and let us never lose sight of the wonder and majesty of the world around us. For in the end, it's not just about the discoveries we make, but the journey itself—the journey of a lifetime."

And with that, they set off into the excavation site, their hearts full of hope and their minds ablaze with the promise of discovery. Together, they would uncover the secrets of the past, rewrite the pages of history, and leave behind a legacy that would endure for generations to come.

As they worked tirelessly, digging through layers of soil and uncovering artifacts long buried beneath the earth, a sense of wonder filled their hearts. Each discovery was a triumph, each revelation a testament to the power of human curiosity and the resilience of the human spirit.

And as they stood amidst the ruins of ancient civilizations, their hands trembling with excitement and their eyes shining with awe, they knew that they were a part of something truly remarkable. They were not just archaeologists or researchers—they were explorers, adventurers, and dreamers, bound together by a common purpose and a shared belief in the power of knowledge to change the world.

And as the sun set on another day of discovery, casting long shadows across the landscape, and painting the sky with hues of orange and gold, Kanchana, Elodie , and Naureen stood together, united in their pursuit of truth and determined to make their mark on the world.

For in the end, it wasn't just about the artifacts or the accolades—it was about the journey itself, the friendships forged along the way, and the indomitable spirit of human curiosity that drove them ever forward, into the unknown, in search of answers that would illuminate the mysteries of the past and illuminate the path to a brighter future.

And as they looked out over the excavation site, their hearts filled with hope and their minds ablaze with the promise of discovery, they knew that their journey was far from over—that the greatest discoveries were still waiting to be made, and that with courage, determination, and a steadfast belief in the power of knowledge, anything was possible.

For in the end, it wasn't just about the artifacts or the accolades—it was about the journey itself, the bonds they formed along the way, and the memories they would carry with them for the rest of their lives. And as they stood together, united in purpose and driven by their shared passion for uncovering the secrets of the past, they knew that there was nothing they couldn't accomplish.

And so, with hearts full of hope and minds open to the wonders of the unknown, they pressed forward, ready to write the next chapter in the story of their lives—a chapter filled with adventure, discovery, and the promise of a future brighter than they could ever imagine.

As they embarked on their journey, Kanchana, Elodie , and Naureen shared a knowing smile, their eyes alight with the thrill of anticipation. The road ahead was uncertain, but one thing was certain— they were ready to make history.

And with that, they set off into the unknown, their hearts filled with hope and their minds ablaze with the promise of discovery.

As they embarked on their journey, Kanchana, Elodie , and Naureen shared a knowing smile, their eyes alight with the thrill of anticipation. The road ahead was uncertain, but one thing was certain— they were ready to make history.

And with that, they set off into the unknown, their hearts filled with hope and their minds ablaze with.

Trio's Diary:

Dear Diary,

Kanchana: Today has been a day of reflection and contemplation. The news of Zayd Hasan's illness weighs heavy on my heart, casting a shadow over our work and reminding me of the fragility of life. Zayd has always been more than just a colleague—he's been a mentor, a friend, and a guiding light in our quest for knowledge. The thought of him facing such a formidable adversary fills me with a sense of helplessness and sorrow. But amidst the darkness, there is a glimmer of hope—the strength of our friendship, the resilience of the human spirit, and the unwavering determination to face whatever challenges lie ahead. As we continue our journey, I find solace in the knowledge that we are not alone, and that together, we can overcome even the greatest of obstacles. And so, as we press forward, I carry Zayd in my thoughts and prayers, holding onto the hope that he will find the courage and strength to fight his battle with grace and dignity.

Elodie : Today has been a day filled with uncertainty and concern. The news of Zayd Hasan's illness has shaken me to the core, reminding me of the frailty of life and the unpredictability of the future. Zayd has always been a steadfast presence in our lives, a source of wisdom and guidance in the face of adversity. To see him grappling with such a formidable foe is both heartbreaking and humbling. Yet, amidst the despair, there is a glimmer of hope—the bond that unites us, the shared determination to stand by Zayd in his time of need. As we navigate the challenges ahead, I find strength in the knowledge that we are not alone, that together, we can weather any storm that comes our way. My thoughts are with Zayd and his family, and I pray that they find solace in the love and support that surrounds them.

Naureen: Today has been a day of introspection and concern. The news of Zayd Hasan's illness has left me grappling with a myriad of emotions, from shock and disbelief to sadness and apprehension. Zayd has always been a pillar of strength and resilience, a mentor and friend who has guided us through some of our darkest moments. To see him facing such a formidable foe is a stark reminder of the fragility of life and the uncertainty of tomorrow. Yet, amidst the turmoil, there is a glimmer of hope—the resilience of the human spirit, the unwavering support of friends, and the belief that together, we can overcome even the greatest of challenges. As we rally around Zayd in his time of need, I find solace in the bonds that unite us, in the shared determination to stand by him every step of the way. My thoughts are with Zayd and his family, and I pray that they find strength and courage in the days ahead.

Chapter 26: The Hidden Library

The weeks following the awards ceremony were a whirlwind of activity for Kanchana, Elodie , and Naureen. Their newfound fame brought an influx of opportunities and challenges. Yet, amidst the excitement, they never lost sight of their primary goal: to continue uncovering hidden truths and making history.

One brisk autumn morning, Kanchana received an unexpected invitation. A letter, sealed with an ornate emblem she didn't recognize, arrived at their headquarters. Inside, a handwritten note read:

"Dear Kanchana Desai, Elodie Laurent, and Naureen Mehra,

Your recent achievements have not gone unnoticed. I invite you to explore a hidden gem within Blackwood Manor—a library that has been concealed for centuries. Within its walls lie texts and artifacts that could reshape our understanding of history. Please join me at the manor at your earliest convenience.

Yours sincerely, Eliza Blackwood"

Kanchana read the letter aloud, her voice filled with excitement. "This could be the breakthrough we've been waiting for."

Elodie nodded, her eyes sparkling with anticipation. "Imagine the treasures we might find there."

Naureen, always the practical one, added, "Let's make sure we're well-prepared. If this library has been hidden for centuries, we might encounter some unexpected challenges."

The trio packed their equipment, ensuring they had everything they might need for the exploration. As they drove to Blackwood Manor, their minds buzzed with possibilities. The recent events and the looming concern for Dr. Hasan added a layer of urgency to their quest. They were determined to uncover as much as they could, hoping that their discoveries might somehow contribute to finding solutions or offering solace.

Upon arrival, Eliza Blackwood greeted them warmly at the grand entrance. Her presence was as commanding as ever, her eyes twinkling with a mix of wisdom and curiosity.

"I'm glad you could come," she said, leading them through the manor's labyrinthine corridors. "The library you're about to see was sealed by my ancestors to protect its contents from those who might misuse the knowledge within. Only a few have known of its existence, and even fewer have entered its sacred space."

They arrived at a heavy oak door, adorned with intricate carvings and a large, ancient lock. Eliza produced an old key, its metal worn smooth by time, and inserted it into the lock. The door creaked open, revealing a dimly lit room filled with the scent of aged paper and leather.

As their eyes adjusted to the low light, Kanchana, Elodie , and Naureen took in the sight before them. Shelves upon shelves of ancient books lined the walls, interspersed with glass cases containing artifacts of varying sizes and shapes. In the centre of the room stood a large wooden table, covered in maps and manuscripts.

"This is incredible," Kanchana whispered, her voice echoing in the hushed space.

Elodie moved toward the nearest shelf, her fingers lightly brushing the spines of the books. "These texts look ancient. Some of them might be one of a kind."

Naureen, drawn to the artifacts, carefully examined a bronze astrolabe housed in one of the cases. "This place is a treasure trove."

Eliza nodded. "Indeed, it is. My hope is that you will be able to unlock the secrets contained within these walls and bring to light the knowledge that has been hidden for so long."

The trio set to work, each of them gravitating toward different areas of the library. Kanchana began deciphering a series of manuscripts written in an archaic script. Elodie focused on cataloguing the various texts, identifying those that might hold the most significant historical value. Naureen meticulously documented the artifacts, taking detailed notes and photographs.

Hours passed in a blur of activity. The sheer volume of information was overwhelming, but their excitement kept them going. As Kanchana delved deeper into one particularly dense manuscript, she stumbled upon a passage that caught her attention.

"Listen to this," she called out to Elodie and Naureen. "It describes a hidden chamber beneath the manor, accessible only through a secret passage in this very library."

Elodie 's eyes widened. "A hidden chamber? That could hold even more treasures." Naureen, ever the sceptic, asked, "But how do we find the passage?"

Kanchana scanned the manuscript, her finger tracing the lines of text. "According to this, there's a mechanism hidden behind a specific book on the third shelf from the left."

They moved to the indicated shelf, their eyes scanning the spines of the books. After a few minutes of searching, Elodie found the book described in the manuscript. With a sense of anticipation, she pulled it slightly toward her. There was a soft click, and a section of the bookshelf swung open, revealing a narrow staircase descending into darkness.

Eliza, who had been observing their efforts with a knowing smile, handed them a lantern. "Be careful. No one has ventured down there in centuries."

With the lantern casting flickering shadows on the walls, the trio descended the staircase, their steps echoing in the confined space. At the bottom, they found a heavy door, its surface etched with intricate patterns.

Naureen pushed it open, and they stepped into a cavernous room. The air was cool and musty, and the walls were lined with shelves holding more books and artifacts. In the centre of the room stood a large stone pedestal, on which rested an ornate chest.

Kanchana approached the chest, her hands trembling with excitement. She lifted the lid, revealing a collection of scrolls, each bound with a silk ribbon.

"These must be the most precious documents," she said, carefully untying one of the scrolls and unrolling it.

The scrolls contained detailed maps, ancient writings, and illustrations of long-forgotten civilizations. As they pored over the documents, a sense of awe and wonder filled the room. They realized they were standing at the threshold of a monumental discovery.

Elodie 's voice was filled with reverence. "This is beyond anything we could have imagined. These scrolls could rewrite entire chapters of history."

Naureen nodded, his expression serious. "We need to document everything meticulously. This knowledge is too important to lose."

As they continued their exploration, they found more hidden compartments and secret passages, each revealing further layers of the manor's rich history. The more they uncovered, the more they realized the significance of their discovery.

But amidst their excitement, a shadow loomed over their thoughts. Zayd Hasan's illness weighed heavily on their minds, a constant reminder of the fragility of life. They were determined to make the most of this opportunity, not just for themselves, but for Zayd, who had always inspired them to seek the truth.

As the day turned into evening, they reluctantly decided to take a break and return to the surface. Eliza, who had been waiting patiently in the library, greeted them with a knowing look.

"You've found something significant, haven't you?" she asked.

Kanchana nodded. "The hidden chamber is incredible. The scrolls and artifacts we found could change our understanding of history."

Eliza smiled, a look of pride and satisfaction on her face. "I'm glad you think so. My ancestors would be pleased to know that their efforts to preserve this knowledge were not in vain."

The trio spent the next few days meticulously documenting their findings, ensuring that every detail was recorded. They contacted experts in various fields to help them analyse the texts and artifacts, eager to unlock the secrets they contained.

As they worked, their thoughts often drifted to Zayd. They knew he would be proud of their discoveries, but they also wished he could be there with them, sharing in the excitement and wonder.

One evening, as they were reviewing their notes, Kanchana received a call from Evelyn. Zayd had been admitted to the hospital again, and his condition had worsened. The news hit them hard, but they were determined to remain strong for their friend.

"We need to finish what we started," Elodie said, her voice resolute. "Zayd would want us to keep going."

Naureen agreed. "Let's make sure our work honours his legacy."

The next morning, they received an unexpected visit from Dr. Hartwell, a renowned historian who had taken an interest in their discoveries. She brought with her a team of experts, eager to assist in the analysis of the scrolls and artifacts.

"Your work has already made waves in the academic community," Dr. Hartwell said. "We're here to help you uncover the full significance of your findings."

With the additional support, their progress accelerated. They uncovered connections between the scrolls and other ancient texts, revealing a complex web of knowledge that spanned continents and centuries.

One of the scrolls contained detailed instructions for constructing a device that could amplify the power of the Gate of Worlds. The implications were staggering. If they could build the device, they might be able to harness the gate's full potential, unlocking even more secrets of the past.

But they also knew the risks involved. The gate was a powerful tool, and misuse could have catastrophic consequences. They needed to proceed with caution, ensuring that their actions were guided by wisdom and integrity.

As they worked tirelessly, they found solace in each other's company. Their shared determination and camaraderie gave them strength, even as they faced the uncertainty of Zayd's condition.

One evening, as they were reviewing their findings, Kanchana received another call from Evelyn. Zayd had taken a turn for the worse, and the doctors were not optimistic about his chances.

The news hit them like a punch to the gut. They knew they needed to be there for their friend, to offer whatever support and comfort they could. They made arrangements to visit Zayd in the hospital the next day, hoping to lift his spirits and let him know how much he meant to them.

As they walked into Zayd's hospital room, they were struck by how frail he looked. But his eyes still held the same spark of intelligence and curiosity that had always inspired them.

"Hey, you guys," Zayd said, his voice weak but filled with warmth. "I hear you've been making history."

Trio's Diary:

Dear Diary, Elodie :

Today has been a whirlwind of emotions. Discovering the hidden library at Blackwood Manor felt like stepping into a dream. The ancient texts and artifacts we found are beyond anything I could have imagined. But even amidst the excitement, the shadow of Zayd's illness looms large. Hearing about his condition worsening has been a stark reminder of the fragility of life. I want to make every discovery count, to honour Zayd and the passion for knowledge he instilled in us. We must press on, not just for history's sake, but for him.

Kanchana:

Exploring the hidden library was an experience I'll never forget. The sense of wonder and awe as we uncovered those ancient scrolls and artifacts was exhilarating. Yet, the joy is bittersweet, knowing that Zayd is fighting such a tough battle. His strength and wisdom have always been our guiding light, and now it's our turn to be strong for him. We're uncovering secrets that could change our understanding of the past, and I hope that in some way, our work brings him comfort and pride. We are determined to see this through, for Zayd and for the legacy of knowledge he values so deeply.

Naureen:

Today was like living in a piece of history. The hidden library at Blackwood Manor was a treasure trove, and the thrill of discovering those ancient texts was incredible. But the news about Zayd's health hit me hard. It's difficult to balance the excitement of our discoveries with the worry and sadness for our friend. Zayd has always been a pillar of strength and inspiration for us. Now, as we push forward with our research and discoveries, we do so with him in our hearts. We need to make every moment count, to honour him with our work and our determination.

Together, we'll face whatever comes next, for the sake of knowledge and for Zayd.

Chapter 27: The Echoes of Emberwood

The sun hung low in the sky, casting long shadows across the rolling hills of Emberwood. The village, steeped in history and surrounded by lush forests, was known for its ancient legends and mysterious ruins. The Emberwood Historical Society had invited Kanchana, Elodie , and Naureen to investigate newly discovered ruins that hinted at a lost civilization predating the Roman era.

As they approached the village, the air was thick with the scent of pine and earth. The trio had barely unpacked when they were greeted by Mr. Harris, the head of the Historical Society, a spry man in his seventies with a passion for local lore.

"Welcome to Emberwood," Mr. Harris said, his eyes twinkling with excitement. "We have much to show you. The ruins we found might change our understanding of this area's history."

The trio followed him through the village, past quaint cottages, and ancient oak trees, to a clearing where the ruins lay. Stone structures, half-buried in the earth, hinted at a once-thriving settlement. Kanchana's eyes widened with curiosity, Elodie 's fingers itched to document everything, and Naureen felt a surge of adrenaline at the thought of uncovering more secrets.

As they began their exploration, Kanchana's mind wandered back to Dr. Hasan. His struggle with cancer was a constant presence in their thoughts, casting a shadow over their excitement. She remembered his words: "Every discovery is a piece of a larger puzzle. Don't let anything stop you from putting those pieces together." She felt a pang of sadness, hoping their work would bring him some solace.

Elodie carefully examined the carvings on a stone pillar, her thoughts also drifting to Zayd. His illness had brought an urgency to their work, a need to uncover and preserve as much as they could. She admired his resilience and determination, and it spurred her on to give her best effort, no Naureener the challenges.

Naureen, meanwhile, was mapping the site with his usual precision, but his thoughts were with Evelyn and Zayd. He knew how much Zayd had influenced their careers and their passion for history. As he worked, he silently promised to make every discovery count, to honour the man who had taught them so much.

The ruins at Emberwood were unlike anything they had encountered before. The architecture was unique, and the artifacts they found—pottery, tools, and remnants of textiles—suggested a highly advanced culture. Kanchana, Elodie , and Naureen worked tirelessly, their focus only interrupted by brief, whispered conversations about Zayd's health.

One afternoon, as they were cataloguing a set of intricately carved stones, Mr. Harris approached them with a parchment in hand. "I found this in the village archives," he said. "It's a map that seems to indicate a hidden chamber beneath the ruins."

The trio's excitement was palpable as they studied the map. Kanchana traced the lines with her finger, her mind racing with possibilities. "If this is accurate, we could be looking at a burial chamber or a treasury. Either way, it could hold significant artifacts."

Elodie nodded, her eyes gleaming. "Let's get to work. This could be the breakthrough we've been looking for."

Following the map, they carefully excavated the area, uncovering a stone entrance sealed with a heavy slab. With great effort, they managed to move the slab, revealing a narrow staircase descending into darkness.

Torches in hand, they descended into the chamber, the air growing cooler and damper with each step. The flickering light revealed walls adorned with murals depicting scenes of daily life, battles, and celestial events. At the far end of the chamber stood a stone sarcophagus, its lid carved with the likeness of a regal figure.

Kanchana's breath caught in her throat. "This is incredible. We've found a tomb of a significant figure from this lost civilization."

Elodie approached the sarcophagus, carefully examining the carvings. "These inscriptions might tell us who this person was and their importance to the society."

Naureen documented everything meticulously, his mind still partially occupied with thoughts of Zayd. He wondered how Zayd would react to their discovery and wished he could be there to share the moment with them.

As they prepared to open the sarcophagus, they paused, each lost in their own thoughts about Dr. Hasan. Kanchana broke the silence, her voice soft but determined. "Let's do this for Zayd. He taught us the value of uncovering history and understanding the past. Let's make him proud."

With a collective nod, they carefully lifted the lid of the sarcophagus. Inside, they found the remains of a noble figure, adorned with intricate jewellery, and surrounded by artifacts of great significance. The discovery was breathtaking, a testament to the advanced and sophisticated nature of the lost civilization.

They spent the following days meticulously documenting and preserving the contents of the tomb. The village of Emberwood buzzed with excitement as news of the discovery spread. Scholars and historians from across the country arrived to witness the findings and offer their expertise.

Throughout it all, Kanchana, Elodie , and Naureen remained focused, driven by their desire to honour Zayd's legacy. They knew that their work in Emberwood would have a lasting impact on the field of archaeology and deepen the understanding of ancient civilizations.

As they prepared to leave Emberwood, Mr. Harris presented them with a plaque from the Historical Society, commemorating their contributions. "You've not only uncovered a piece of our past but also inspired a renewed passion for history in our community," he said.

Kanchana, Elodie , and Naureen thanked him, their hearts full of gratitude and a renewed sense of purpose. They knew their journey was far from over, and they were determined to continue their work, driven by the memory of Zayd and the knowledge that they were making a difference.

As they travelled back to their headquarters, their thoughts returned to Zayd. They hoped their discoveries would bring him some measure of joy and pride, knowing that his teachings and guidance had led them to such significant findings.

The road ahead was uncertain, but they faced it with a steadfast resolve. Together, they would continue to uncover the mysteries of the past, driven by the desire to make history and honour the legacy of their dear friend and mentor.

Trio's Diary:

Dear Diary, Elodie :

Today's discovery at Emberwood has been one of the most profound experiences of my career. Uncovering the hidden chamber and the ancient tomb felt like stepping back in time. But even amid this excitement, I can't help but think of Zayd. His strength and wisdom have guided us to this point, and I hope he knows how much he means to us. We're doing this for him, to honour his legacy and make him proud.

Kanchana:

Finding the hidden chamber at Emberwood has been an incredible journey. The artifacts and inscriptions we've uncovered are beyond anything I could have imagined. Yet, amidst the thrill of discovery, Zayd's illness is always on my mind. His teachings and passion for history have shaped who we are as researchers. I hope that our work brings him some comfort and pride.

We're determined to continue our quest for knowledge, driven by his enduring influence.

Naureen:

Today's discovery at Emberwood has been nothing short of amazing. The hidden chamber and the tomb of a noble figure have opened a new chapter in our understanding of ancient civilizations. But as I document each artifact, I can't help but think of Zayd. His guidance and support have been our foundation. We're pushing forward with our work, determined to make every discovery count, not just for history's sake, but for him.

Chapter 28: Secrets of the Night Sky

The night sky over Ravenshire was clear, a blanket of stars stretching endlessly above the ancient stone circle. Kanchana, Elodie , and Naureen stood at the edge of the circle, their equipment laid out in neat rows. Tonight, they were returning to the place where their journey had truly begun, ready to delve deeper into the mysteries of the Gate of Worlds.

Kanchana adjusted the settings on her camera, preparing to document the celestial alignment that they hoped would reveal more secrets of the ancient site. "I've always wondered if there's more to these stones than we've already discovered," she mused, her eyes reflecting the twinkling stars above.

Elodie , examining a star map, nodded. "If the patterns on these stones correspond to specific celestial events, we might uncover something extraordinary tonight."

Naureen, setting up a telescope, glanced at his friends. "Do you ever think about how far we've come since we first discovered the Gate? And how much of that is because of Zayd?"

Their thoughts turned to Dr. Zayd Hasan, whose battle with cancer weighed heavily on their minds. His wisdom and guidance had been instrumental in their work, and they were determined to continue making discoveries that would honour his legacy.

As the trio waited for the stars to align, they discussed their recent findings and the significance of their work. Kanchana's mind drifted to Zayd, recalling the times he had inspired them with his passion for uncovering the past. She hoped their efforts would bring him some measure of comfort and pride.

The minutes ticked by, and the stars gradually moved into position. The ground beneath them began to hum with energy, and the stones of Ravenshire Ring glowed faintly. Kanchana captured every moment on her camera, while Elodie meticulously noted the changes in her journal.

"This is it," Naureen said, his voice filled with awe. "The stones are responding to the alignment."

As the celestial event reached its peak, a beam of light shot from the central stone into the sky, illuminating a hidden pattern of constellations. The trio watched in wonder as the light traced an intricate design across the heavens, revealing a map of sorts, connecting Ravenshire Ring to other ancient sites around the world.

Kanchana's heart raced with excitement. "This is incredible! It's a network of ancient sites, all connected by celestial alignments."

Elodie added, "If we can decode this map, we could unlock countless secrets of the past. This might be the key to understanding the Gate of Worlds on a global scale."

Naureen nodded, his mind racing with possibilities. "We need to document everything and compare it with the data we've collected from other sites. This could be the breakthrough we've been searching for."

As the celestial event concluded and the light faded, the trio began their analysis, piecing together the information revealed by the stars. They worked late into the night, driven by their shared passion and the desire to honour Zayd's teachings.

In the early hours of the morning, as the first light of dawn crept over the horizon, they finally paused to reflect on their findings. Kanchana looked at her friends, her eyes shining with determination. "We've uncovered something monumental tonight. This is just the beginning of a new chapter in our research."

Elodie smiled, feeling a renewed sense of purpose. "Zayd would be proud of what we've achieved. We need to keep pushing forward, no Naureener the challenges."

Naureen agreed, his voice steady. "We're in this together, and we'll make sure every discovery counts. For Zayd, and for the legacy of the Gate of Worlds."

As they packed up their equipment and prepared to head back to their headquarters, their thoughts lingered on Zayd. They knew his time might be limited, but his influence would continue to guide them in their quest for knowledge. They were more determined than ever to make history, not just by uncovering the past, but by forging a legacy that would endure for generations to come.

Their journey was far from over, and they faced it with unwavering resolve. Together, they would unlock the mysteries of the ancient world, driven by the desire to honour the man who had inspired them and to ensure that his teachings would live on in every discovery they made.

Trio's Diary:

Dear Diary, Elodie :

Tonight was a reminder of why we do what we do. As we stood beneath the stars at Ravenshire Ring, I couldn't help but think of Zayd. His passion for uncovering the past has always driven us, and tonight, we made a discovery that would have made him proud. The celestial alignment revealed a network of ancient sites, all connected by the stars. It feels like we've taken a huge step forward in understanding the Gate of Worlds. I hope Zayd knows how much his guidance means to us.

Kanchana:

The energy at Ravenshire Ring was palpable tonight. As the stars aligned and the stones began to glow, I felt a surge of excitement and awe. We've always known there was more to this place, and tonight, we uncovered a hidden map in the sky. It's moments like these that remind me of Zayd and his unwavering belief in our work. Despite his illness, I hope he finds solace in knowing that his teachings continue to inspire us and drive our discoveries.

Naureen:

Standing under the night sky at Ravenshire Ring, watching the stones come to life, was nothing short of magical. The celestial event revealed a map of connected ancient sites, a breakthrough we've been searching for. Zayd has been on my mind a lot lately, especially with his health declining. I know he would have been thrilled by our discovery tonight. We're determined to keep pushing forward, not just for the sake of history, but to honour Zayd and the legacy he's helped us build.

Chapter 29: The Guardians' Path

The next few weeks were a whirlwind of activity and emotion for Kanchana, Elodie , and Naureen. The discovery at Ravenshire Ring had propelled them into the spotlight of the archaeological world, attracting attention from scholars and media alike. But as they basked in the excitement of their groundbreaking find, their thoughts frequently returned to Dr. Zayd Hasan and his battle with

cancer. The trio resolved to dedicate their work to him, drawing strength from their mentor's enduring influence.

One crisp autumn morning, as they gathered in their study to review their findings, Kanchana received a

phone call from Eliza Blackwood. Her voice, though aged, carried an urgent tone that immediately set Kanchana on edge.

"I need you to come to Blackwood Manor immediately," Eliza said. "There is something you must see."

Without hesitation, Kanchana relayed the message to Elodie and Naureen. They grabbed their coats and notebooks, their minds racing with possibilities. Blackwood Manor had always been a place of mystery and revelation, and they couldn't afford to miss whatever Eliza had discovered.

The drive to Blackwood Manor was quiet, each of them lost in thought. As they approached the grand estate, the familiar sight of the ivy-clad stone walls and towering turrets brought a sense of

anticipation. Eliza greeted them at the door, her eyes sharp and focused.

"Follow me," she instructed, leading them to the manor's library.

The library, with its towering bookshelves and rich mahogany furnishings, felt like a sanctuary of knowledge. Eliza guided them to a table where an ancient manuscript lay open, its pages filled with delicate, flowing script.

"This," Eliza said, pointing to the manuscript, "is a record of the Guardians' Path."

Kanchana, Elodie , and Naureen leaned in, their curiosity piqued. The Guardians' Path was a legendary journey that ancient protectors of the Gate of Worlds undertook to safeguard its secrets. According to the manuscript, the path was a series of trials and locations that tested the guardians' wisdom, courage, and unity.

Eliza continued, "I believe you three are destined to walk this path. Each location holds a key to understanding the full power of the Gate. You have already unlocked the first secret at Ravenshire Ring. Now, it's time to continue your journey."

The trio exchanged determined looks. They knew this was their calling, a mission that transcended mere historical inquiry. It was a quest to preserve and protect the world's most ancient mysteries.

"Where do we start?" Naureen asked, his voice filled with resolve.

Eliza smiled faintly. "The next location is an ancient temple in the mountains of Greece. The Temple of Oracles."

With their next destination set, the trio wasted no time in preparing for their journey. They booked
    their flights, gathered their equipment, and ensured their research was meticulously organized. As they packed, thoughts of Dr. Hasan lingered in their minds. They hoped their discoveries would bring him
    some measure of joy and pride, even as he faced his own battle.

The flight to Greece was long but filled with a sense of purpose. They arrived in Athens and rented a car, driving through the picturesque countryside to the remote mountains where the Temple of Oracles was said to be hidden. The journey was arduous, with winding roads and steep cliffs, but their
    determination never wavered.

Finally, they reached a small village at the base of the mountains. The locals, intrigued by their mission, directed them to a narrow path leading up to the temple. Armed with their gear and an unyielding resolve, Kanchana, Elodie , and Naureen began the climb.

The path was treacherous, with loose rocks and dense underbrush. As they ascended, the air grew

thinner, and the landscape more rugged. But the sight of the ancient temple, perched high on a rocky ledge, spurred them on.

The Temple of Oracles was a marvel of ancient architecture, with towering columns and intricate

carvings depicting scenes of prophecy and guidance. The air was thick with the scent of pine and the whispers of history. As they entered the temple, a sense of reverence washed over them.

Inside, they found a central chamber adorned with mosaics and statues. In the centre of the room stood a stone pedestal, upon which rested a crystal sphere. The sphere pulsed with a faint, ethereal light.

"This must be the Oracle's Eye," Kanchana said, her voice hushed with awe.

Elodie nodded, her eyes fixed on the sphere. "According to the manuscript, the Oracle's Eye is said to reveal visions of the past and future. But it requires a test of spirit to activate."

Naureen stepped forward, his expression resolute. "Let's do this together."

They joined hands, forming a circle around the pedestal. Closing their eyes, they focused their thoughts and energy, channelling their collective willpower into the Oracle's Eye. The sphere began to glow brighter, and a soft hum filled the air.

Suddenly, their minds were flooded with visions. They saw ancient guardians standing where they stood, their faces etched with determination and purpose. They witnessed the creation of the Gate of Worlds, the merging of realms, and the trials that each guardian faced. Among these visions, they saw themselves, walking the same path, connected by a timeless legacy.

As the visions faded, the sphere's light dimmed, leaving the trio breathless and overwhelmed.

"Did you see that?" Kanchana whispered, her voice trembling with emotion.

Elodie nodded, tears glistening in her eyes. "We're part of something much bigger than ourselves. We're continuing a legacy that spans millennia."

Naureen, his face pale but determined, said, "And we'll honour that legacy, no Naureener what."

With newfound understanding and resolve, they carefully took the Oracle's Eye and made their way back down the mountain. The journey had been taxing, but the sense of accomplishment and purpose fuelled their every step.

Returning to the village, they were greeted by curious locals who had heard of their venture. The trio shared their experience, feeling a deep connection to the people who lived in the shadow of the temple.

As they sat in a small taverna, enjoying a meal and reflecting on their journey, their thoughts inevitably turned to Dr. Hasan. They knew he would be proud of their discovery, and they hoped to share their experiences with him soon.

The following days were filled with travel and preparation for their next destination. Each step they took felt like a tribute to Zayd, whose teachings and guidance had led them to this moment. The Guardians' Path was far from complete, but they were ready to face whatever challenges lay ahead.

Their next clue led them to an ancient library in Alexandria, Egypt, where they sought the Scroll of Ages, said to contain knowledge from civilizations long lost to time. The library was a labyrinth of corridors and towering shelves filled with ancient texts and scrolls.

Guided by their determination and the manuscript's clues, they navigated the library's vast collections. The Scroll of Ages was hidden in a secret chamber, protected by a series of intricate puzzles that tested their knowledge and teamwork.

As they solved each puzzle, their minds flashed back to Zayd, whose love for history and discovery had inspired their quest. His battle with cancer weighed heavily on them, but it also fuelled their determination to succeed.

Finally, they uncovered the Scroll of Ages, its ancient parchment filled with detailed accounts of civilizations that had once wielded the power of the Gate of Worlds. The scroll provided crucial insights into how the Gate was used and the consequences of its misuse.

With the scroll in hand, they felt a profound sense of accomplishment. They had not only uncovered a piece of history but also made history themselves. Their discoveries would contribute to the world's understanding of ancient civilizations and their connection to the Gate.

As they left the library, their hearts were heavy with the knowledge that Zayd's time was limited. They vowed to share their findings with him as soon as possible, hoping to bring him some measure of joy and pride in his final days.

Returning to their headquarters, they meticulously documented their discoveries, preparing to present their findings to the world. Their research attracted the attention of leading scholars and institutions, culminating in a prestigious award ceremony where they were honoured for their contributions to archaeology and history.

The ceremony was a bittersweet moment. As they accepted their awards and accolades, their thoughts were with Zayd, whose influence had shaped their journey. They knew he would have been proud of their achievements and the legacy they were building.

As they stood on the stage, surrounded by applause and admiration, Kanchana, Elodie , and Naureen felt a deep sense of fulfilment. They had not only honoured Zayd's teachings but also ensured that his legacy would live on through their work.

Returning to their headquarters, they gathered around a table filled with their notes and artifacts. The journey ahead was still uncertain, but they were ready to face it together, united by their shared mission and the memory of their beloved mentor.

Their thoughts turned to the future and the challenges that lay ahead. The Guardians' Path was a
daunting journey, filled with trials and discoveries that would test their resolve and unity. But they were determined to honour Zayd's legacy and continue their quest, no Naureener where it led them.

As they prepared for their next adventure, their hearts were filled with hope and determination. The road ahead was long and uncertain, but they knew they could face it together, drawing strength from their bond and the knowledge that they were part of something much greater than themselves.

Together, they would navigate the intricate web of history, uncovering the mysteries of the Gate of Worlds and safeguarding its secrets for future generations. Their journey was far from over, but they were ready to face whatever challenges lay ahead, guided by the memory of Dr. Zayd Hasan and the legacy he had inspired.

Trio's Diary:

Dear Diary,

Elodie :
Today's ceremony was a deeply emotional experience. Standing on that stage, receiving the award for our discoveries, I couldn't help but think of Dr. Hasan. His guidance and wisdom have been our cornerstone, and I wish he could have been there to see the culmination of his

teachings. The knowledge we've gained and the history we've uncovered are all tributes to his legacy. I hope our work brings him some measure of pride and comfort in his battle with

cancer. The road ahead is daunting, but with Zayd in our hearts, we can face anything.

Kanchana:
Accepting the award today was an honour, but it was also bittersweet. Zayd's absence was palpable, and I found myself wishing he could have shared in our moment of triumph. His battle with cancer is a constant reminder of life's fragility, but it also drives us to make the most of every opportunity. The discoveries we've made are not just for us—they're for him and for all the wisdom he imparted to us. As we continue on the Guardians' Path, I am

determined to honour his legacy in everything we do.

Naureen:

Today was a reminder of how far we've come and how much we've achieved, but also of the challenges that still lie ahead. Dr. Hasan's fight with cancer has been a heavy weight on our hearts, and I hope that our success brings him some comfort. Our journey has only just begun, and I am more determined than ever to ensure that our work honours his legacy. We owe so much to him, and as we continue on the Guardians' Path, I know that his spirit will guide us. The future is uncertain, but with Elodie and Kanchana by my side, and Zayd in our thoughts, I believe we can overcome any obstacle.

Chapter 30: The Last Wish

The crisp autumn air carried a sense of urgency as Kanchana, Elodie , and Naureen gathered at their Victorian headquarters. The past few months had been a whirlwind of discoveries and accolades, but beneath their achievements lay a shared worry: Dr. Zayd Hasan's
deteriorating health. Despite his courageous battle with cancer, Zayd had grown weaker, and the trio felt an increasing need to visit him.

One afternoon, they received an unexpected call from Evelyn. Her voice, usually strong, was tinged with sadness and resolve.

"Zayd wants to see you," she said. "He has something important to share."

The trio exchanged concerned glances but didn't hesitate. They packed their things and set off for the hospital, their hearts heavy with anticipation.

As they entered Zayd'ss room, they were struck by how frail he looked. His once-vibrant eyes were dimmer, and his movements slower. But his smile, warm and welcoming, was
unchanged.

"Ah, my favourite adventurers," Zayd greeted them. "Come, sit with me."

They gathered around his bed, each taking a hand. Zayd looked at each of them in turn, his gaze filled with a mixture of pride and sorrow.

"I've watched you grow from eager students into accomplished historians," he began. "You've made incredible discoveries, but there's one more journey you must undertake."

Kanchana, always the most perceptive, sensed the gravity of his words. "What is it, Zayd?"

He took a deep breath. "There's a hidden chamber beneath Blackwood Manor. It contains a final artefact, one that could unlock untold secrets about our world's history. I've kept its existence a secret, but I believe it's time for you to find it."

Elodie 's eyes widened. "A hidden chamber? Why haven't you told us about it before?"

Zayd smiled wistfully. "Some secrets are best kept until the right moment. And now, with my time running short, I want to ensure this knowledge is passed on to those who will use it wisely."

Naureen, his voice thick with emotion, asked, "How do we find it?"

Zayd handed them a worn leather journal. "This journal contains the clues you'll need. Follow them, and you'll find the chamber. But promise me one thing: use what you find for the greater good. Don't let it fall into the wrong hands."

They nodded solemnly, each feeling the weight of his words.

"We promise," Kanchana said softly.

Zayd leaned back, his eyes closing briefly. When he opened them again, they were filled with a gentle determination. "I believe in you. Now, go and make history."

With that, they bid him farewell, each carrying a piece of his legacy with them.

Back at Blackwood Manor, the trio stood in the grand foyer, the journal in Kanchana's hands. The manor, with its ivy-clad walls and ancient aura, felt different now—more alive, filled with the echoes of the past.

Kanchana opened the journal, reading aloud the first clue: "In the room where ancestors gaze, seek the lion's silent roar."

Elodie glanced at the portraits lining the walls. "The ancestors must be these portraits. But what's the lion's silent roar?"

Naureen, his eyes scanning the room, spotted an intricately carved lion on the fireplace mantle. "Over there!"

They hurried to the fireplace, examining the lion. Behind its carved mouth, Kanchana found a small lever. She pulled it, and a section of the wall slid open, revealing a narrow staircase leading down.

With lanterns in hand, they descended into the darkness. The air grew cooler, the musty scent of age surrounding them. At the bottom, they found a heavy wooden door adorned with ancient runes.

Kanchana traced her fingers over the symbols. "These runes speak of knowledge and protection. This is it."

They pushed the door open, revealing a vast chamber filled with artifacts and scrolls. In the centre stood a pedestal, upon which rested a crystalline sphere, pulsating with a soft blue
light.

Elodie approached the pedestal, her voice reverent. "This must be the artifact Zayd mentioned."

Naureen nodded. "It's beautiful. But what does it do?"

Kanchana, her eyes reflecting the sphere's glow, said, "I think it's a key—to unlocking the past and protecting the future."

As they carefully placed the sphere in a secure case, Kanchana's phone buzzed. It was a message from Evelyn.

"Zayd passed peacefully," it read. "His last words were about you. He said, 'They will make history.'"

Tears filled their eyes as they stood in the hidden chamber, the weight of Zayd'ss last wish settling over them. They knew their journey was far from over. The discoveries they had

made were only the beginning, and now, armed with the knowledge and the final artefact, they were ready to continue their quest.

Trio's Memoir:

Elodie :
Zayd'ss passing left a void in my heart that nothing can fill. However, his last wish
bestowed upon me a renewed sense of purpose. As we stood in that hidden chamber, I could almost feel his presence guiding us. We have a responsibility now—not just to uncover
history but to protect it. Zayd believed in us, and I am determined not to let him down.

Kanchana:
The discovery of the hidden chamber was a bittersweet triumph. It stands as a testament to Zayd'ss faith in us and his unwavering dedication to preserving history. As we move
forward, I carry his legacy with me, determined to honour his memory through our work. The artifact we found is more than just a key; it symbolizes the profound trust Zayd placed in us.

Naureen:
The discovery at Blackwood Manor was a moment of triumph shadowed by sorrow. Zayd'ss last wish has infused me with a renewed sense of duty. I am more determined than ever to
ensure our work honours his legacy. The path ahead is uncertain, but with Elodie and Kanchana by my side, I know we can face any challenge. For Zayd, we will make history.

In remembering Zayd, we acknowledge the depth of his impact on our lives and work. His vision for our mission has become our guiding star, leading us through the darkest moments. Together, we are not just a team of historians—we are the guardians of his dream, entrusted with the legacy of uncovering and safeguarding the truths of the past. Each step we take is in his honour, each discovery a tribute to his memory.

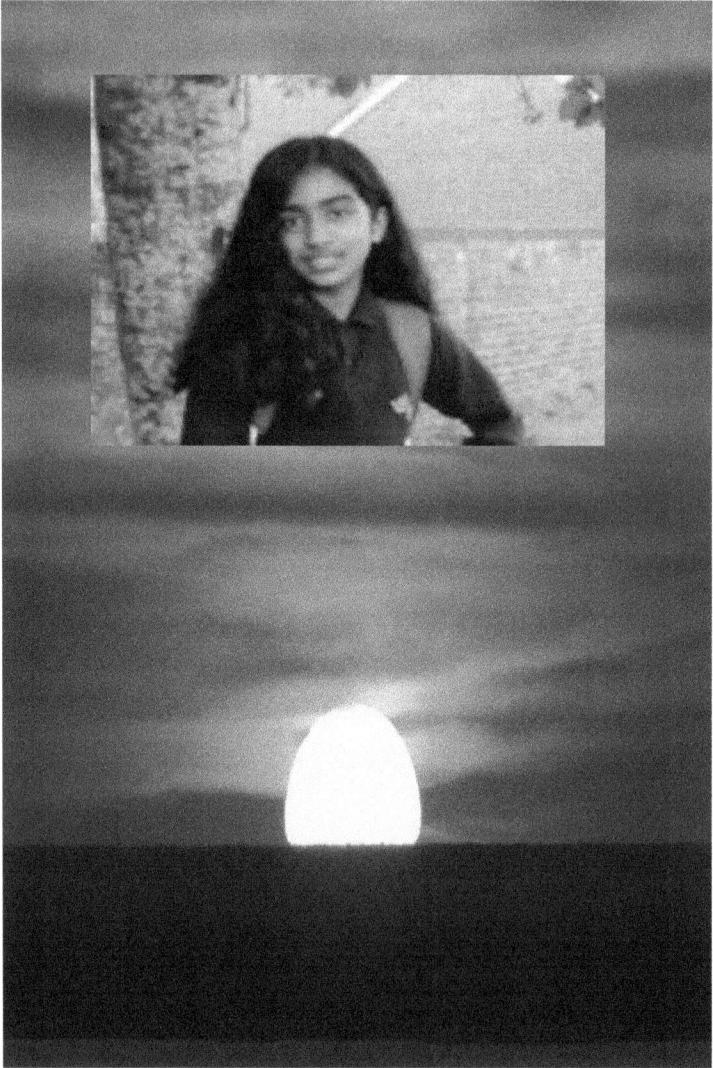

Danika, a 13-year-old bookworm, has always been passionate about reading and writing. As she delved deeper into her studies, her love for learning only grew stronger. She spent hours devouring books of all genres, and soon discovered that she had a knack for storytelling herself. With the encouragement of her teachers and family, Danika began writing her own tales, weaving intricate plots and characters that came alive on the page. Her hard work paid off when she published her first book, "Once Upon Historians", a historical fiction novel that combines her love of reading and learning.

Through writing, Danika finds solace and escape from the stresses of everyday life, using her words as a tool to cope with her emotions and process her thoughts. With "Once Upon Historians" under her belt, Danika is determined to continue pursuing her dreams and inspiring others to do the same. Danika, a 13-year-old bookworm, has always been passionate about reading and writing. As she delved deeper into her studies, her love for learning only grew stronger. She spent hours devouring books of all genres, and soon discovered that she had a knack for storytelling herself. With the encouragement of her teachers and family, Danika began writing her own tales, weaving intricate plots and characters that came alive on the page. Her hard work paid off when she

published her first book, "Once Upon Historians", a historical fiction novel that combines her love of reading and learning. Through writing, Danika finds solace and escape from the stresses of everyday life, using her words as a tool to cope with her emotions and process her thoughts. With "Once Upon Historians" under her belt, Danika is determined to continue pursuing her

dreams and inspiring others to do the same.

Welcome to the History Realm, where Elodie , Naureen and Kanchana conquer and make History.

Dive into a world where the secrets of the past hold the keys to the

future. In "Once Upon Historians," follow the gripping adventures of Kanchana, Elodie , and Naureen, undercover historians on a quest to uncover the mysteries of history's most enigmatic artifacts and lost civilizations.

From the bustling factories of the Industrial Revolution to the hidden chambers of Blackwood Manor, their journey takes them across time and space, confronting sinister adversaries and unlocking the secrets of ancient lore.

Guided by mentors and fuelled by friendship, they push the boundaries of discovery, unearthing truths that have remained hidden for

centuries.

But as they face their greatest challenges yet, they must confront their pasts and embrace the legacy they carry, for the fate of history itself hangs in the balance.

Join Kanchana, Elodie , and Naureen on an epic adventure filled with intrigue, danger, and the enduring power of friendship.

Also by Danika Prasad

Meanwhile, Elsewhere
Invitation to Paris
Once Upon Historians

About the Author

Danika, a 13-year-old bookworm, has always been passionate about reading and writing. As she delved deeper into her studies, her love for learning only grew stronger. She spent hours devouring books of all genres, and soon discovered that she had a knack for storytelling herself. With the encouragement of her teachers and family, Danika began writing her own tales, weaving intricate plots and characters that came alive on the page. Her hard work paid off when she published her first book, "Once Upon Historians", a historical fiction novel that combines her love of reading and learning. Through writing, Danika finds solace and escape from the stresses of everyday life, using her words as a tool to cope with her emotions and process her thoughts. With "Once Upon Historians" under her belt, Danika is determined to continue pursuing her dreams and inspiring others to do the same. Danika, a 13-year-old bookworm, has always been passionate about reading and writing. As she delved deeper into her studies, her love for learning only grew stronger. She spent hours devouring books of all genres, and soon discovered that she had a knack for storytelling herself. With the encouragement of her teachers and family, Danika began writing her own tales, weaving intricate plots and characters that came alive on the page. Her hard work paid off when she published her first book, "Once Upon Historians", a historical fiction novel that combines her love of reading and learning. Through writing, Danika finds solace and escape from the stresses of everyday life, using her words as a tool to cope with her emotions and process her thoughts. With "Once Upon Historians" under her belt, Danika is determined to continue pursuing her dreams and inspiring others to do the same.